TREASURE ISLAND

— Robert Louis —
Stevenson

TREASURE
ISLAND

PETER HADDOCK PUBLISHING

Published in this edition 1997 by Peter Haddock Publishing,
United Kingdom
Reprinted 1999, 2004

© 1997 This arrangement, text and illustrations,
Geddes & Grosset, David Dale House,
New Lanark, Scotland

© Original text John Kennett

Illustrated by Mike Lacey (Simon Girling Associates)

ISBN 0 7105 0933 2

Printed and bound in Poland

Contents

To the Reader

I am sure you will have seen a film, or watched a programme on TV, that has been made from some famous book. If you enjoyed the film or programme, you may have decided to read the book.

Then what happens? You get the book and, it's more than likely, you get a shock as well! You turn ten or twenty pages, and nothing seems to *happen*. Where are all the lively people and exciting incidents? When, you say, will the author get down to telling the story? In the end you will probably throw the book aside and give it up. Now, why is that?

Well, perhaps the author was writing for adults and not for children. Perhaps the book was written a long time ago, when people had more time for reading and liked nothing better than a book that would keep them entertained for weeks.

We think differently today. That's why I've taken some of these wonderful books, and retold them for you. If you enjoy them in this shorter form, then I hope that when you are older you will go back to the original books, and enjoy all the more the wonderful stories they have to tell.

About the Author

Robert Louis Stevenson, novelist, essayist, and poet, was born in Edinburgh in 1850. Although he never enjoyed good health, he travelled widely, finally making his home in the tropical island of Samoa, where he died in 1894.

His poems for children are collected in *A Child's Garden of Verses*. Among his many tales of adventure, *Catriona* is of especial interest to readers of this book, since in it he tells of further adventures of David Balfour.

Chapter One

The Old Sea Dog
at the Admiral Benbow

Squire Trelawney, Dr Livesey, and the rest of the company asked me to write down the story of our adventure on Treasure Island, from the beginning to the end, keeping nothing back but the location of the island, and that only because there is still treasure remaining there. And so, many years later, I begin to write of the year when I became fourteen, when my father kept the Admiral Benbow Inn and the old seaman with the scarred face first took up his lodging under our roof.

I remember him as if it were yesterday, as he came plodding to the inn door, pulling his sea chest behind him in a barrow. He was a tall, strong, heavy, man, with his hair tied in a pigtail falling over the shoulders of his dirty blue coat. His hands were ragged and scarred, with black, broken nails, and the scar across one cheek shone from his dirty face as a livid white. As he came, I remember he kept looking round the bay and whistling to himself as he did so. He then sang, in his high, old, wavering voice, that old sea song that he sang so often afterwards:

"Fifteen men on the dead man's chest—
Yo-ho-ho, and a bottle of rum!"

Then he rapped on the door with a bit of stick like a handspike that he carried, and when my father appeared, called roughly for a glass of rum. When this was brought to him, he savoured it slowly and looked about him at the cliffs and up at our sign-board. After some time he spoke:

"This is a handy cove," he said, "do you get many people passing through, mate?"

"No, I'm sorry to say." said my father, "It's a lonely spot all year round."

"Well, then," said he, "this is the place for me. Here you, matey," he cried to the man who trundled the barrow; "bring that up alongside and help me with my chest. I'll stay here a bit," he continued. "I'm a plain man; rum and bacon and eggs is what I want, and that headland there to watch for ships. What's your name boy?"

"My name is Jim Hawkins, sir. Will you tell me what I might call you?"

"What you might call me? You might call me Captain. Oh, I see what you're at. Don't worry about paying—I'll pay all right," and he threw down three or four gold pieces in front of me. "Tell me when I've spent that and give me a glass of rum," he said, looking as fierce as a commander.

Despite his dirty clothes and his coarse way of speaking, he seemed like a man who was accustomed to being obeyed. The man who came with the barrow told us that the coach had set him down the morning before at the Royal George, that he had asked if there were any inns along the coast, and hearing ours well spoken of, I suppose, and described as lonely, had chosen it from the others for his place of residence. And that was all we could learn of our guest.

He was a strange, silent man. All day he hung round the cove or upon the cliffs with a brass telescope; all evening he sat in a corner of the parlour next the fire and drank rum and water. Mostly he would not speak when spoken to, but would look up

suddenly and fiercely and blow through his nose like a foghorn.

We and the people who came to the inn soon learned to leave him alone.

Every day when he came back from his stroll he would ask if any sailors had gone by along the road. At first we thought he was keen to have the company of his own kind, but at last we began to see he was anxious to avoid them. When a seaman stayed at the Admiral Benbow, he would look in at him through the curtained door before he entered the parlour; and he was always sure to be as silent as a mouse when a sailor was present.

One day he took me aside and promised me a silver fourpenny on the first of every month if I would only keep my "weather eye open for a seafaring man with one leg" and let him know the moment he appeared. Often enough when the first of the month came round and I asked him for my wage, he would only blow through his nose at me and stare me down. But before the week ended he was sure to think again and decide to bring me my fourpenny piece, and repeat his orders to look out for "the seafaring man with one leg."

How the man with one leg haunted my dreams, I need scarcely tell you. On stormy nights, when the wind shook the four corners of the house and the surf roared along the cove and up the cliffs, I would imagine him in a thousand forms, and with a thousand wicked expressions. I would see him with the leg cut off at the knee, then at the hip. He would become a monstrous kind of a creature who had only ever had one leg, and that in the middle of his body. To see him leap and run and pursue me over hedge and ditch was the worst of nightmares. And altogether I think I earned my monthly fourpenny piece, in the shape of these terrible dreams.

But though I was so terrified by the idea of the seafaring man with one leg, I was far less afraid of the captain himself than anybody else who knew him. There were nights when he drank too much rum and water and then he would sometimes sit and sing his wicked, old, wild sea songs, taking no notice of anyone. But sometimes he would force all the trembling company to listen to his stories or sing the chorus to his sea-songs. Often I have heard the house shaking with "Yo-ho-ho, and a bottle of rum," all the neighbours joining in for dear life, with the fear of death upon them, and each singing louder than the other.

So the days and weeks passed, and the captain still stayed with us. It worried my father a lot. He thought that other people would stop coming to the inn because of the captain. The weeks became months and the captain never paid a penny more than those first few gold pieces. If my father mentioned the money he owed us the captain just glared at him.

All the time he lived with us the captain made no change whatever in his dress except to buy some stockings from a peddlar. I remember the appearance of his coat, which he patched himself upstairs in his room, and which, before the end, was nothing but patches. He never wrote or received a letter, and he never spoke with anyone except the neighbours, and even then, for the most part, only when he was drunk on rum. None of us had ever seen the contents of the great sea chest he owned.

Only once did anyone stand up to him, and that was towards the end, when my poor father was very ill and becoming worse. Dr Livesey came late one afternoon to see the patient. My mother made him some dinner and he went into the parlour to smoke a pipe until his horse returned from the hamlet, for we had no stabling at the inn. I followed him in, and I remember observ-

ing the contrast that the neat, bright doctor, with skin as white
as snow and bright, black eyes and pleasant manners, made with
the country folk that came to the inn, and above all, with that
filthy, heavy, drunken scarecrow of a pirate of ours, sitting, drinking his rum, with his arms on the table. Suddenly he—the captain, that is—began to pipe up his eternal song:

"Fifteen men on the dead man's chest—Yo-ho-ho, and a bottle of rum!

Drink and the devil had gone for the rest—Yo-ho-ho, and a
bottle of rum!"

At first I had supposed "the dead man's chest" to be that iden-
tical big box of his upstairs in the front room, and the thought
had been mingled in my nightmares with that of the one-legged
seafaring man. But by this time we had all long ceased to pay
any particular notice to the song. This song was new, that night,
to Dr Livesey, and I observed it did not produce an agreeable
effect on him, for he looked up for a moment quite angrily before he went on with his talk to old Taylor, the gardener, on a
new cure for the rheumatics. In the meantime, the captain gradually brightened up at his own music, and at last flapped his hand
upon the table before him in a way we all knew to mean silence.
The voices stopped at once, all but Dr Livesey's; he went on as
before, speaking clear and kind and drawing briskly at his pipe
between every word or two. The captain glared at him for a while,
flapped his hand again, glared still harder, and at last broke out
with a villainous, low oath, "Silence, there, between decks!"

"Were you addressing me, sir?" said the doctor. And when the
ruffian had told him that this was so, the doctor replied "I have
only one thing to say to you, sir, that if you keep on drinking
rum, the world will soon be quit of a very dirty scoundrel!"

The old fellow's fury was awful. He sprang to his feet, drew and opened a knife, and threatened to pin the doctor to the wall.

The doctor never so much as moved. He spoke to him as before, over his shoulder and in the same tone of voice, rather high, so that all the room might hear, but perfectly calm and steady: "If you do not put that knife in your pocket this instant, I promise, upon my honour, that you shall hang."

Then followed a battle of looks between them, but the captain soon knuckled under, put up his weapon, and resumed his seat, grumbling like a beaten dog.

"And now, sir," continued the doctor, "since I now know there's such a fellow in my district, you may expect that I'll have an eye upon you day and night. I'm a magistrate as well as a doctor; and if I catch a breath of complaint against you, even if it's only for a piece of behaviour like tonight's, I'll have you hunted down and turned out of this inn. Now let me hear no more."

Soon after, Dr Livesey's horse came to the door and he rode away, but the captain said no more that evening, and for many evenings to come.

Chapter Two

Black Dog Appears and Disappears

It was not very long after this that there occurred the first of the mysterious events that rid us at last of the captain, though not, as you will see, of his affairs. It was a bitter cold winter, with

long, hard frosts and heavy gales; and it was plain from the beginning that my poor father did not have long to live. He deteriorated daily, and my mother and I had the whole inn to run on our own. We were kept so busy that we did not pay much notice to our unpleasant guest.

Mother was upstairs with father and I was laying the breakfast table for the captain's return, when the parlour door opened and a stranger stepped in. He was a thin, pale creature, with two fingers missing from his left hand, and though he wore a cutlass, he did not look much like a fighter. I had been keeping watch for seafaring men, with one leg or two, and I remember this one puzzled me. He was not sailorly, and yet he had a air of the sea about him too.

I asked him what I could get for him, and he said he would take rum but as I was going out of the room to fetch it, he sat down upon a table and motioned me to come towards him. I paused where I was, with my napkin in my hand.

"Come here, sonny," he said. "Come nearer here." I took a step nearer.

"Is this here table for my mate Bill?" he asked.

I told him I did not know his mate Bill, and this was for a person who stayed in our house whom we called the captain.

"Well," said he, "my mate Bill would be called the captain, as like as not. He has a cut on one cheek and a mighty pleasant way with him, particularly in drink, has my mate Bill. We'll put it, for argument's sake, that your captain has a cut on one cheek—and we'll put it, if you like, that the cheek's the right one. Ah, well! I told you. Now, is my mate Bill in this here house?"

I told him that he was out walking.

"Which way, sonny? Which way is he gone?"

And when I had pointed out the rock and told him what way the captain was likely to return, and how soon, and answered a few other questions, he said, "Ah, this'll be as good as drink to my mate Bill, when he sees that I'm here."

There was an unpleasant look on his face as he said these words, and I had my own reasons for thinking that the stranger was mistaken, even supposing he meant what he said. The stranger kept hanging about just inside the inn door, peering round the corner like a cat waiting for a mouse. Once I stepped out into the road, but he immediately called me back, and when I did not obey quickly enough for his liking, a most horrible change came over his face, and he ordered me in with an oath that made me jump. As soon as I was back again he returned to his former manner, half fawning, half sneering.

"The great thing for boys is discipline, sonny—discipline." said he, "Now, if you had been on a ship with Bill, he wouldn't have had to speak to you twice. That was never Bill's way, nor the way of such that sailed with him. And here, sure enough, is my mate Bill, with a spyglass under his arm, bless his old 'art, to be sure. You and me'll just go back into the parlour, sonny, and get behind the door, and we'll give Bill a little surprise—bless his 'art, I say again."

The stranger backed along with me into the parlour and put me behind him in the corner so that we were both hidden by the open door. I was very uneasy and alarmed, as you can imagine, and it rather added to my fears to observe that the stranger was certainly frightened himself. He cleared the hilt of his cutlass and loosened the blade in the sheath and all the time we were waiting there he kept swallowing as if he felt what we used to call a lump in the throat.

At last in strode the captain, slammed the door behind him, without looking to the right or left, and marched straight across the room to where his breakfast awaited him.

"Bill," said the stranger in a voice that I thought he had tried to make bold and big.

The captain spun round on his heel and faced us. All the colour had gone from his face, and even his nose was blue. He had the look of a man who has seen a ghost and I felt sorry to see him all of a sudden turn so old and sick.

"Come, Bill, you know me; you know an old shipmate, Bill, surely," said the stranger.

The captain made a sort of gasp.

"Black Dog!" said he.

"And who else?" replied the other, getting more at his ease. "Black Dog, come for to see his old shipmate Billy, at the Admiral Benbow Inn. Ah, Bill, Bill, we have seen a sight of times, us two, since I lost them two talons," holding up his mutilated hand.

"Now, look here," said the captain; "you've found me. Here I am. Well, then, speak up; what is it?"

"That's you, Bill," returned Black Dog, "you're in the right of it, Billy. I'll have a glass of rum from this dear child here, who I've took such a liking to and we'll sit down, if you please, and talk square, like old shipmates."

When I returned with the rum, they were already seated on either side of the captain's breakfast table.

Black Dog sat next to the door, sideways so as to have one eye on his old shipmate and one, I thought, on his means of escape.

He asked me go and leave the door wide open. "None of your keyholes for me, sonny," he said; and I left them together and retired into the bar.

For a long time, though I certainly did my best to listen, I could hear nothing but a low gabbling, but at last the voices began to grow higher, and I could pick up a word or two, mostly curses, from the captain.

"No, no, no, no; and an end of it!" he cried once. And again, "If it comes to hanging, we'll all hang, I say."

Then all of a sudden there was a tremendous explosion of shouting, cursing and other noises—the chair and table went over in a lump, a clash of steel followed, and then a cry of pain, and the next instant I saw Black Dog in full flight, and the captain hotly pursuing, both with drawn cutlasses, and the former streaming blood from the left shoulder. Just at the door the captain aimed at the fugitive one last tremendous cut, which would certainly have split him in half had it not been intercepted by our big signboard of Admiral Benbow. You may see the notch on the lower side of the frame to this day.

That blow was the last of the battle. Once out upon the road, Black Dog, in spite of his wound, disappeared over the edge of the hill in half a minute. The captain, for his part, stood staring at the signboard like a bewildered man. Then he passed his hand over his eyes several times and at last turned back into the house.

"Jim," he said, "rum"; and as he spoke, he reeled a little, and caught himself with one hand against the wall.

"Are you hurt?" I cried.

"Rum," he repeated. "'I must get away from here. Rum! Rum!"

I ran to fetch it, but I was quite unsteadied by all that had fallen out, and I broke one glass and fouled the tap, and while I was still getting in my own way, I heard a loud fall in the parlour, and running in, saw the captain lying full length upon the floor. At the same instant my mother, alarmed by the cries and

fighting, came running downstairs to help me. Between us we raised his head. He was breathing very loud and hard, but his eyes were closed and his face was a horrible colour.

"Dear, deary me," cried my mother, "what a disgrace upon the house! And your poor father sick!"

In the meantime, we had no idea what to do to help the captain. It was a happy relief for us when the door opened and Doctor Livesey came in, on his visit to my father.

"Oh, doctor," we cried, "what shall we do? Where is he wounded?"

"Wounded? A fiddlestick's end!" said the doctor. "No more wounded than you or I. The man has had a stroke, as I warned him. Now, Mrs. Hawkins, just you run upstairs to your husband and tell him, if possible, nothing about it. For my part, I must do my best to save this fellow's worthless life."

The doctor ripped up the captain's sleeve and exposed his great sinewy arm. It was tattooed in several places. "Here's luck", "A fair wind", and "Billy Bones his fancy", were very neatly and clearly executed on the forearm; and up near the shoulder there was a sketch of a gallows and a man hanging from it—done, as I thought, with great spirit.

"Prophetic," said the doctor, touching this last picture with his finger. "Jim," he said, "are you afraid of blood?"

"No, sir," said I.

"Well, then," said he, "you hold the basin." And with that he took his lancet and opened a vein.

A great deal of blood was taken before the captain opened his eyes and looked mistily about him. First he recognized the doctor with an unmistakable frown. Then his glance fell upon me, and he looked relieved. But suddenly his colour changed, and he tried to raise himself, crying, "Where's Black Dog?"

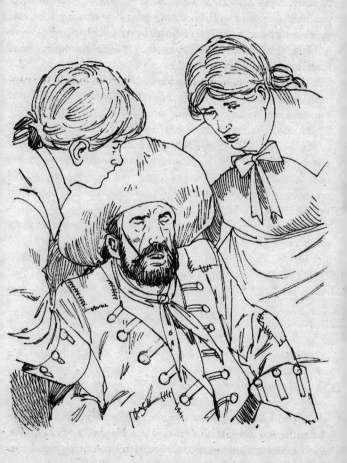

"There is no Black Dog here," said the doctor, "except what you have on your own back. You have been drinking rum and you have had a stroke, precisely as I told you. I have just, very much against my own will, dragged you head foremost out of the grave. Now, Mr Bones—"

"That's not my name," he interrupted.

"I don't much care," returned the doctor. "It's the name of a buccaneer of my acquaintance and I call you by it for the sake of shortness. What I have to say to you is this: one glass of rum won't kill you, but if you take one you'll take another and another, and I stake my wig if you don't stop you'll die—do you understand that?"

Between us, with great difficulty, we managed to hoist him upstairs, and laid him on his bed.

The doctor went off to see my father, taking me with him by the arm.

Chapter Three

The Black Spot

About noon I stopped at the captain's door with some cooling drinks and medicines.

"Jim," he said, "you're the only one here that's worth anything, and you know I've been always good to you. Never a month has passed without me giving you a silver fourpenny for yourself. And now you see, mate, I'm pretty low, deserted and alone. Jim, you'll bring me one noggin of rum, now, won't you, matey?"

"The doctor—" I began.

But he broke in cursing the doctor, in a feeble voice but heartily. "Doctors is all swabs," he said; "and that doctor there, why,
what do he know about seafaring men? I been in places hot as
pitch, and mates dying with Yellow Jack, and the land a-heav-
ing like the sea with earthquakes—what do the doctor know of
lands like that?—and I lived on rum, I tell you. It's been meat
and drink, and man and wife, to me; and if I'm not to have my
rum my blood'll be on you, Jim, and that doctor swab," and he
ran on again for a while with curses. "Look, Jim, how my fingers fidges," he continued in the pleading tone. "I can't keep
'em still, not I.

I haven't had a drop this blessed day. That doctor's a fool, I tell
you. If I don't get my rum, Jim, I'll have the horrors. I seen
some already. I seen old Flint in the corner there, behind you as
plain as print, I seen him. If I get the horrors, I'm a man that
has lived rough, and I'll raise Cain. Your doctor hisself said one
glass wouldn't hurt me. I'll give you a golden guinea for a noggin, Jim."

He was growing more and more excited, and this alarmed me
for my father's sake. Father was very ill that day and needed
quiet. Besides, I was reassured by the doctor's words, now quoted
to me, and rather offended by the offer of a bribe.

"I want none of your money," I said, "I only want what you
owe my father. I'll get you one glass, and no more."

When I brought it, he seized it greedily and drank it out.

"Aye, aye," said he, "that's better, sure enough. And now, did
that doctor say how long I was to lie here in this old berth?"

"A week at least," I said.

"Thunder!" he cried. "A week! I can't do that; they'd have the
black spot on me by then. The lubbers is going about to get the

wind of me this blessed moment; lubbers who couldn't keep what they got, and want to steal what belongs to another. Is that seamanly behaviour, now, I want to know? But I'm a saving soul. I never wasted good money of mine, nor lost it neither; and I'll trick 'em again. I'm not afraid of 'em. I'll shake out another reef, matey, and fool 'em again."

As he was thus speaking, he had risen from bed with great difficulty, holding to my shoulder with a grip that almost made me cry out, and moving his legs like they were a dead weight. His words, spirited as they were in meaning, contrasted sadly with the weakness of the voice with which they were uttered. He paused when he had got into a sitting position on the edge.

"That doctor's done me," he murmured. "My ears is singing. Lay me back."

Before I could do much to help him he had fallen back again to his former place, where he lay for a while silent.

"Jim," he said at length, "you saw that seafaring man today?"

"Black Dog?" I asked.

"Ah! Black Dog," says he. "He's a bad un; but there's worse than him that are looking for me. It's my old sea chest they're after. Now, if I can't get away, and they tip me the black spot, you get on a horse—you can ride can't you?—well, then, you get on a horse, and go to that eternal doctor swab, and tell him to pipe all hands—magistrates and such—and he'll lay 'em aboard at the Admiral Benbow—all old Flint's crew, man and boy, all of 'em that's left. I was first mate, I was—old Flint's first mate, and I'm the only one who knows the place. He gave it to me at Savannah, when he lay dying, you see. But you won't peach unless they get the black spot on me, unless you see that Black Dog again or a seafaring man with one leg, Jim—him above all."

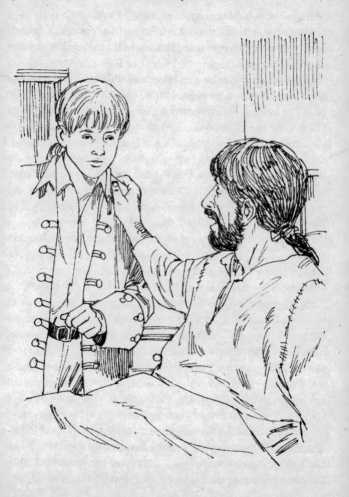

"But what is the black spot, captain?" I asked.

'That's a summons, mate. I'll tell you if they get that. But you keep your weather eye open, Jim, and I'll give you equal share, upon my honour."

He wandered a little longer, his voice growing weaker; but soon after I had given him his medicine, which he took like a child, he fell at last into a heavy, swoon-like sleep, in which I left him. What I should have done, had all gone well, I do not know. Probably I should have told the whole story to the doctor, for I was in mortal fear that the captain might regret telling me what he had and kill me. But I did not think any more that night about his strange words because my poor father died quite suddenly that evening, which put all other matters on one side. Our natural distress, the visits of the neighbours, the arranging of the funeral, and all the work of the inn to be carried on meanwhile kept me so busy that I had scarcely time to think of the captain, far less to be afraid of him.

He was downstairs the next morning and had his meals as usual, though he ate little and had more, I am afraid, than his usual supply of rum, for he helped himself out of the bar, scowling and blowing through his nose, and no one dared to cross him. On the night before the funeral he was as drunk as ever. It was shocking, in that house of mourning, to hear him singing away at his ugly old sea song, but weak as he was, we were all in the fear of death for him, and the doctor was suddenly taken up with a case many miles away and was never near the house after my father's death. I have said the captain was weak, and indeed he seemed instead to grow weaker than regain his strength. He clambered up and down stairs, and went from the parlour to the bar and back again, and sometimes put his nose out of doors

to smell the sea, holding on to the walls as he went for support and breathing hard and fast like a man on a steep mountain. He never particularly addressed me—and it is my belief he had as good as forgotten his confidences—but his temper was more flighty, and allowing for his bodily weakness, more violent than ever. He had an alarming way now when he was drunk of drawing his cutlass and laying it bare before him on the table. But with all that, he noticed people less and seemed shut up in his own thoughts and rather wandering. Once, for instance, to our extreme wonder, he piped up a different tune, a kind of country love song that he must have learned in his youth before he had begun to follow the sea.

So things passed until, the day after the funeral, and about three o'clock of a bitter foggy, frosty afternoon, I was standing at the door for a moment, full of sad thoughts about my father, when I saw someone drawing slowly near along the road. He was plainly blind, for he tapped before him with a stick and wore a great green shade over his eyes and nose; and he was hunched, as if with age or weakness, and wore a huge old tattered sea cloak with a hood that made him appear positively deformed. I never saw in my life a more dreadful-looking figure. He stopped a little from the inn, and raising his voice in an odd singsong, addressed the air in front of him, "Will any kind friend inform a poor blind man, who has lost the precious sight of his eyes in the gracious defence of his native country, England—and God bless King George!—where or in what part of this country he may now be?"

"You are at the Admiral Benbow, Black Hill Cove, my good man," said I.

"I hear a voice," said he, "a young voice. Will you give me

your hand, my kind young friend, and lead me in?" I held out my hand, and the horrible, soft-spoken, eyeless man gripped it in a moment like a vice. I was so much startled that I struggled to withdraw, but the blind man pulled me close up to him with a single action of his arm.

"Now, boy," he said, "take me to the captain."

"Sir," said I, "upon my word I dare not."

"Oh," he sneered, "that's it! Take me in straight or I'll break your arm."

And he gave my arm a wrench that made me cry out.

"Sir," said I, "I only mean to warn you for your own safety. The captain is not what he used to be. He sits with a drawn cutlass. Another gentleman—"

"Come, now, march," he interrupted. I never heard a voice so cruel, and cold, and ugly as that man's. It frightened me more than the pain, and I began to obey him at once, walking straight in the door and towards the parlour, where our sick old buccaneer was sitting, dazed with rum. The blind man clung close to me, holding me with one iron fist and leaning almost more of his weight on me than I could carry.

"Lead me straight up to him, and when I'm in view, cry out 'Here's a friend for you, Bill.' If you don't I'll do this," and with that he gave my arm a twist that I thought would have made me faint.

I was so utterly terrified of the blind beggar that I forgot my terror of the captain, and as I opened the parlour door, cried out the words he had ordered in a trembling voice.

The poor captain raised his eyes, and with one look at the blind beggar became suddenly sober. The expression on his face was not so much of terror as of mortal sickness. He made a

movement to rise, but I do not believe he had enough force left in his body.

"Now, Bill, sit where you are," said the beggar. "If I can't see, I can hear a finger stirring. Business is business. Hold out your left hand—boy, take his left hand by the wrist and bring it near to my right."

We both obeyed him to the letter, and I saw him pass something from the hollow of the hand in which he held his stick into the palm of the captain's, which closed upon it instantly.

"And now that's done," said the blind man. And at the words he suddenly let me go, and with incredible accuracy and nimbleness, skipped out of the parlour and into the road, where, as I still stood motionless, I could hear his stick go tap-tap-tapping into the distance.

It was some time before either I or the captain seemed to gather our senses, but at length, and about at the same moment, I released his wrist, which I was still holding, and he drew in his hand and looked sharply into the palm.

"Ten o'clock!" he cried. "Six hours. We'll do them yet," and he sprang to his feet.

Even as he did so, he reeled, put his hand to his throat, stood swaying for a moment, and then, with a peculiar sound, fell from his whole height face-down on the floor.

I ran to him at once, calling to my mother. But haste was all in vain. The captain had been struck dead. It is a curious thing to understand, for I had certainly never liked the man, though of late I had begun to pity him, but as soon as I saw that he was dead, I burst into a flood of tears. It was the second death I had known, and the sorrow of the first was still fresh in my heart.

Chapter Four
The Sea Chest

I had lost no time, of course, in telling my mother all that I knew, and perhaps should have told her long before, and we knew at once that we were in a difficult and dangerous position. Some of the man's money—if he had any—was certainly owed to us, but it was not likely that our captain's shipmates, above all the two specimens seen by me, Black Dog and the blind beggar, would be inclined to give up their booty to pay the dead man's debts. The captain's order to mount at once and ride for Dr Livesey would have left my mother alone and unprotected, which was not to be thought of. Indeed, it seemed impossible for either of us to remain much longer in the house. The fall of coals in the kitchen grate, the very ticking of the clock, filled us with fear. The neighbourhood, to our ears, seemed haunted by approaching footsteps. Between the dead body of the captain on the parlour floor and the thought of that detestable blind beggar hovering near at hand and ready to return, there were moments when, as the saying goes, I jumped out of my skin with terror. Something must speedily be decided upon, and it occurred to us at last to go together and seek help in the neighbouring hamlet. No sooner said than done. Bareheaded as we were, we ran out at once in the gathering evening and the frosty fog.

The hamlet lay not many hundred yards away, though out of view, on the other side of the next cove, and what greatly en-

couraged me was that it was in the opposite direction from where the blind man had made his appearance and had presumably returned. We were not many minutes on the road, though we sometimes stopped to make sure we were in reach of each other and to listen. But there was no unusual sound—nothing but the low wash of the ripple and the croaking of the inhabitants of the wood.

It was already darkening when we reached the hamlet, and I shall never forget how much I was cheered to see the yellow shine of doors and windows; but that, as it proved, was the best help we were likely to get in that area. For—you would have thought men would have been ashamed of themselves—no soul would agree to return with us to the Admiral Benbow. The more we told of our troubles, the more—man, woman, and child—they clung to the shelter of their houses. The name of Captain Flint, though it was strange to me, was well known to some there and carried a great weight of terror. Some of the men who had been to find work on the far side of the Admiral Benbow remembered having seen several strangers on the road, and taking them to be smugglers, ran away. One at least had seen a little ship in what we called Kitt's Hole. For that matter, anyone who was a comrade of the captain's was enough to frighten them to death. And the short and the long of the matter was, that while we could get several who were willing enough to ride to Dr Livesey's, which lay in another direction, not one would help us to defend the inn.

They say cowardice is infectious, but then argument is, on the other hand, a great emboldener; and so when each had said his say, my mother made them a speech. She would not, she declared, lose money that belonged to her fatherless boy.

"If none of the rest of you dare," she said, "Jim and I dare. Back we will go, the way we came, and small thanks to you big, hulking, chickenhearted men. We'll have that chest open, if we die for it. And I'll thank you for that bag, Mrs Crossley, to bring back our lawful money in."

Of course I said I would go with my mother, and of course they all cried out at our foolhardiness, but even then not a man would go along with us. All they would do was to give me a loaded pistol lest we were attacked, and to promise to have horses ready saddled in case we were pursued on our return, while one lad was to ride ahead to the doctor's in search of armed assistance.

My heart was beating hard when we two set forth in the cold night upon this dangerous venture. A full moon was beginning to rise and peered redly through the upper edges of the fog, and this increased our haste, for it was plain, before we came forth again, that all would be as bright as day, and our departure exposed to the eyes of any watchers. We slipped along the hedges, noiseless and swift, nor did we see or hear anything to increase our terrors, till, to our relief, the door of the Admiral Benbow had closed behind us.

I slipped the bolt at once, and we stood and panted for a moment in the dark, alone in the house with the dead captain's body. Then my mother got a candle in the bar, and holding each other's hands, we advanced into the parlour. He lay as we had left him, on his back, with his eyes open and one arm stretched out.

"Draw down the blind, Jim," whispered my mother; "they might come and watch outside. And now," she said when I had done so, "we have to get the key off that," and she pointed to the body of the dead captain. "And who's to touch it, I should

like to know!" and she gave a kind of sob as she said the words.

I went down on my knees at once. On the floor close to his hand there was a little round piece of paper, blackened on the one side. I could not doubt that this was the black spot and taking it up, I found written on the other side, in a very good, clear hand, this short message: "You have till ten tonight."

"He had till ten, mother," said I; and just as I said it, our old clock began striking. This sudden noise startled us shockingly; but the news was good, for it was only six.

"Now, Jim," she said, "that key."

I felt in his pockets, one after another. A few small coins, a thimble, and some thread and big needles, a piece of pigtail tobacco bitten away at the end, his gully with the crooked handle, a pocket compass, and a tinder box were all that they contained, and I began to despair.

"Perhaps it's round his neck," suggested my mother.

Overcoming a strong feeling of disgust, I tore open his shirt at the neck, and there, sure enough, hanging to a bit of tarry string, which I cut with his own knife, we found the key. At this triumph we were filled with hope and hurried upstairs without delay to the little room where he had slept so long and where his box had stood since the day of his arrival.

It was like any other seaman's chest on the outside, the initial "B" burned on the top of it with a hot iron and the corners somewhat smashed from a long rough journey.

"Give me the key," said my mother; and though the lock was stiff, she had turned it and thrown back the lid in a twinkling.

A strong smell of tobacco and tar rose from the interior, but nothing was to be seen on the top except a suit of very good clothes, carefully brushed and folded. They had never been worn,

my mother said. Under that there lay various bits and pieces that the captain had kept to remind him of his years at sea: several sticks of tobacco, two very handsome pistols, a piece of bar silver, an old Spanish watch and some other trinkets of little value and mostly of foreign make, a pair of compasses mounted with brass, and five or six curious West Indian shells. I have often wondered since why he should have carried these shells with him in his wandering, guilty, and hunted life.

In the meantime, we had found nothing of any value but the silver and the trinkets, and neither of these were of use to us. Underneath there was an old boat cloak, whitened with sea salt on many a harbour bar. My mother pulled it up with impatience, and there lay before us, the last things in the chest, a bundle tied up in oilcloth looking like papers, and a canvas bag that produced, at a touch, the jingle of gold.

"I'll show these rogues that I'm an honest woman," said my mother. "I'll have only what is owed to me, and nothing more. Hold Mrs Crossley's bag." And she began to count over the amount of the captain's score from the sailor's bag into the one that I was holding.

It was a difficult business, for the coins were of all countries and sizes—doubloons, louis d'ors, guineas, and pieces of eight, and other besides that I did not recognise, all shaken together at random. My mother knew how to make her count only with the guineas although these were by far the scarcest.

When we were about halfway through, I suddenly put my hand upon her arm, for I had heard in the silent, frosty air a sound that brought my heart into my mouth—the tap-tapping of the blind man's stick upon the frozen road. It drew nearer and nearer, while we sat holding our breath. Then it struck sharp on the inn

door, and then we could hear the handle being turned and the
bolt rattling as the wretched being tried to enter. Then there
was a long time of silence both inside and outside. At last the
tapping started again, and, to our indescribable joy and grati-
tude, died slowly away again until it ceased to be heard.

"Mother," I said, "take all the coins and let's be going," for I
was sure the bolted door must have seemed suspicious and would
bring the whole hornet's nest about our ears, though how thank-
ful I was that I had bolted it.

But my mother, frightened as she was, would not consent to
take a fraction more than was due to her and was obstinately
unwilling to be content with less. It was not yet seven, she said,
by a long way. She knew her rights and she would have them;
and she was still arguing with me when a little low whistle
sounded a good way off upon the hill. That was enough, and
more than enough, for both of us.

"I'll take what I have," she said, jumping to her feet.

"And I'll take this to square the count," I said, picking up the
oilskin packet.

Next moment we were both groping downstairs, leaving the
candle by the empty chest, and the next we had opened the
door and were in full retreat. We had not started a moment too
soon. The fog was rapidly dispersing. Already the moon shone
quite clear on the high ground on either side; and it was only in
the exact bottom of the dell and round the tavern door that a
thin veil still hung unbroken to conceal the first steps of our
escape. Far less than halfway to the hamlet, very little beyond
the bottom of the hill, we would have to come forth into the
moonlight. We could already hear the sound of several footsteps running, and as we looked back in their direction, we saw

the light of a lantern tossing to and fro and still rapidly advancing.

"My dear," said my mother suddenly, "take the money and run on. I am going to faint."

This was certainly the end of both of us, I thought. How I cursed the cowardice of the neighbours; how I blamed my poor mother for her honesty and her greed, for her past foolhardiness and present weakness! We were just at the little bridge, by good fortune and I helped her, tottering as she was, to the edge of the bank, where, sure enough, she gave a sigh and fell on my shoulder. I do not know how I found the strength to do it at all, and I am afraid it was roughly done, but I managed to drag her down the bank and a little way under the arch. I could not move her any farther, for the bridge was too low to let me do more than crawl below it. So there we had to stay—my mother almost entirely exposed and both of us within earshot of the inn.

Chapter Five

The Last of the Blind Man

My curiosity, in a sense, was stronger than my fear, for I could not remain where I was, but crept back to the bank again, from where, sheltering my head behind a bush of broom, I might watch the road before our door. I was scarcely in position when my enemies began to arrive, seven or eight of them, running hard, their feet beating out of time along the road and the man with the lantern some paces in front. Three men ran together, hand in hand, and I made out, even through the mist, that the

middle man of this trio was the blind beggar. The next moment his voice showed me that I was right.

"Down with the door!" he cried.

"Aye, aye, sir!" answered two or three and a rush was made upon the Admiral Benbow, the lantern-bearer following. And then I could see them pause, and hear speeches passed in a lower key, as if they were surprised to find the door open. But the pause was brief, for the blind man again issued his commands. His voice sounded louder and higher, as if he were afire with eagerness and rage.

"In, in, in!" he shouted, and cursed them for their delay.

Four or five of them obeyed at once, two remaining on the road with the formidable beggar. There was a pause, then a cry of surprise, and then a voice shouting from the house, "Bill's dead."

But the blind man swore at them again for their delay.

"Search him, some of you shirking lubbers, and the rest of you go upstairs and get the chest," he cried.

I could hear their feet rattling up our old stairs, so that the house must have shook with it. Promptly afterwards, fresh sounds of astonishment arose. The window of the captain's room was thrown open with a slam and a jingle of broken glass, and a man leaned out into the moonlight, head and shoulders, and addressed the blind beggar on the road below him.

"Pew," he cried, "they've been before us. Someone's turned the chest out alow and aloft."

"Is it there?" roared Pew.

"The money's there."

The blind man cursed the money.

"Flint's fist, I mean," he cried.

"We don't see it here nohow," returned the man.

"Here, you below there, is it on Bill?" cried the blind man again.

At that another fellow, probably him who had remained below to search the captain's body, came to the door of the inn. "Bill's been overhauled a'ready," said he; "nothin' left."

"It's these people of the inn—it's that boy. I wish I had put his eyes out!" cried the blind man, Pew. "They were here no time ago—they had the door bolted when I tried it. Scatter, lads, and find 'em."

"Scatter and find 'em! Rout the house out!" reiterated Pew, striking with his stick upon the road.

Then there followed a great to-do through all our old inn, heavy feet pounding to and fro, furniture thrown over, doors kicked in, until the very rocks re-echoed and the men came out again, one after another, on the road and declared that we were nowhere to be found. And just then the same whistle that had alarmed my mother and myself over the dead captain's money was once more clearly audible through the night, but this time twice repeated. I had thought it to be the blind man's trumpet, so to speak, summoning his crew to the assault, but I now found that it was a signal from the hillside towards the hamlet, and from its effect upon the buccaneers, a signal to warn them of approaching danger.

"There's Dirk again," said one. "Twice! We'll have to budge, mates."

"Budge, you skulk!" cried Pew. "Dirk was a fool and a coward from the first—you wouldn't mind him. They must be close by; they can't be far; you have your hands on it. Scatter and look for them, dogs! Oh, shiver my soul," he cried, "if I had eyes!"

This appeal seemed to produce some effect, for two of the fellows began to look here and there among the lumber, but half-heartedly, I thought, and with half an eye to their own danger all the time, while the rest stood irresolute on the road.

"You have your hands on thousands, you fools, and you hang a leg! You'd be as rich as kings if you could find it, you know it's here, and you stand there skulking. There wasn't one of you dared face Bill, and I did it—a blind man! And I'm to lose my chance for you! I'm to be a poor, crawling beggar, sponging for rum, when I might be rolling in a coach! If you had the pluck of a weevil in a biscuit you would catch them still."

"Hang it, Pew, we've got the doubloons!" grumbled one.

"They might have hid the blessed thing," said another. "Take the Georges, Pew, and don't stand here squalling."

Squalling was the word for it; Pew's anger rose so high at these objections till at last, his passion completely taking the upper hand, he struck at them right and left in his blindness and his stick sounded heavily on more than one.

These, in their turn, cursed back at the blind miscreant, threatened him in horrid terms, and tried in vain to catch the stick and wrest it from his grasp.

This quarrel was the saving of us, for while it was still raging, another sound came from the top of the hill on the side of the hamlet—the tramp of horses galloping. Almost at the same time a pistol shot, flash and report, came from the hedge side. And that was plainly the last signal of danger, for the buccaneers turned at once and ran, separating in every direction, one seaward along the cove, one slant across the hill, and so on, so that in half a minute not a sign of them remained but Pew. Him they had deserted, whether in sheer panic or out of revenge for his ill

words and blows I know not; but there he remained behind, tapping up and down the road in a frenzy, and groping and calling for his comrades. Finally he took the wrong turn and ran a few steps past me, towards the hamlet, crying, "Johnny, Black Dog, Dirk," and other names, "you won't leave old Pew, mates— not old Pew!"

Just then the noise of horses topped the rise, and four or five riders came in sight in the moonlight and swept at full gallop down the slope.

At this Pew saw his error, turned with a scream, and ran straight for the ditch, into which he rolled. But he was on his feet again in a second and made another dash, now utterly bewildered, right under the nearest of the coming horses.

The rider tried to save him, but in vain. Down went Pew with a cry that rang high into the night; and the four hoofs trampled him and passed by. He fell on his side, then gently collapsed upon his face and moved no more.

I leaped to my feet and hailed the riders. They were pulling up, at any rate, horrified at the accident and I soon saw what they were. One, tailing out behind the rest, was a lad that had gone from the hamlet to Dr Livesey's; the rest were revenue officers, whom he had met by the way, and with whom he had had the intelligence to return at once. Some news of the ship in Kitt's Hole had found its way to Supervisor Dance and set him forth that night in our direction, and to that circumstance my mother and I owed our lives.

Pew was dead, stone dead. As for my mother, when we had carried her up to the hamlet, a little cold water and salts and that soon brought her back again, and she was none the worse for her terror, though she still continued to deplore her loss of

the rest of the money. In the meantime the supervisor rode on, as fast as he could, to Kitt's Hole; but his men had to dismount and grope down the dingle, leading, and sometimes supporting, their horses, and in continual fear of ambushes; so it was no great matter for surprise that when they got down to the Hole the ship was already leaving, though still close in. He hailed the ship. A voice replied, telling him to keep out of the moonlight or he would get be shot, and at the same time a bullet whistled close by his arm. Soon after, the ship disappeared out of sight.

I went back with him to the Admiral Benbow, and you cannot imagine a house in such a state; the very clock had been thrown down by these fellows in their furious hunt after my mother and myself; and though nothing had actually been taken away except the captain's money bag and a little silver from the till, I could see at once that we were ruined. Mr Dance could make nothing of the scene.

"They got the money, you say? Well, then, Hawkins, what were they after? More money, I suppose?"

"No, sir; not money, I think," I replied. "In fact, sir, I believe I have the thing in my breast pocket; and to tell you the truth, I should like someone to have it in their safekeeping."

"To be sure, boy; quite right," said he. "I'll take it, if you like."

"I thought perhaps Dr Livesey," I began.

"Perfectly right," he interrupted very cheerily, "perfectly right—a gentleman and a magistrate. And, now I come to think of it, I might as well ride round there myself and report to him or squire. Master Pew's dead, when all's done; not that I regret it, but he's dead, you see, and people will make it out against an officer of his Majesty's revenue, if make it out they can. Now, I'll tell you, Hawkins, if you like, I'll take you along."

I thanked him heartily for the offer, and we walked back to the hamlet where the horses were. By the time I had told mother of my purpose they were all in the saddle.

"Dogger," said Mr Dance, "you have a good horse; take up this lad behind you."

As soon as I was mounted, holding on to Dogger's belt, the supervisor gave the word, and the party struck out at a bouncing trot on the road to Dr Livesey's house.

Chapter Six

The Captain's Papers

We rode hard all the way till we drew up before Dr Livesey's door. The house was all dark to the front.

Mr Dance told me to jump down and knock, and Dogger gave me a stirrup to descend by. The door was opened almost at once by the maid.

"Is Dr Livesey in?" I asked.

No, she said, he had come home in the afternoon but had gone up to the hall to dine and pass the evening with the squire.

"So there we go, boys," said Mr Dance.

This time, as the distance was short, I did not mount, but ran with Dogger's stirrup leather to the lodge gates and up the long, leafless, moonlit avenue to where the white line of the hall buildings looked on either hand on great old gardens. Here Mr Dance dismounted, and taking me along with him, was admitted at a word into the house.

The servant led us down a matted passage and showed us at

the end into a great library, all lined with bookcases and busts upon the top of them, where the squire and Dr Livesey sat, pipe in hand, on either side of a bright fire.

I had never seen the squire so near at hand. He was a tall man, over six feet high, and broad in proportion, and he had a bluff, red face, all roughened and lined from his long travels. His eyebrows were very black, and moved readily, and this gave him a look of some temper, not bad, you would say, but quick and high.

"Come in, Mr Dance," says he, very stately and condescending.

"Good evening, Dance," says the doctor with a nod. "And good evening to you, friend Jim. What good wind brings you here?"

The supervisor stood up straight and stiff and told his story like a lesson; and you should have seen how the two gentlemen leaned forward and looked at each other. When they heard how my mother went back to the inn, Dr Livesey fairly slapped his thigh, and the squire cried "Bravo!" and broke his long pipe against the grate. Long before it was done, Mr Trelawney (that, you will remember, was the squire's name) had got up from his seat and was striding about the room, and the doctor, as if to hear the better, had taken off his powdered wig and sat there looking very strange indeed with his own close-cropped black hair.

At last Mr Dance finished the story.

"Mr Dance," said the squire, "you are a very noble fellow. And as for riding down that atrocious criminal, I regard it as an act of virtue, sir, like stamping on a cockroach. This lad Hawkins is a trump, I perceive. Hawkins, will you ring that bell? Mr Dance must have some ale."

"And so, Jim," said the doctor, "you have the thing that they were after, have you?"

"Here it is, sir," said I, and gave him the oilskin packet.

The doctor looked it all over, as if his fingers were itching to open it; but instead of doing that, he put it quietly in the pocket of his coat.

"Squire," said he, "when Dance has had his ale he must, of course, be off on his Majesty's service, but I mean to keep Jim Hawkins here to sleep at my house, and with your permission, I propose we should have serve him up some cold pie and let him eat."

"As you will, Livesey," said the squire; "Hawkins has earned better than cold pie."

So a big pigeon pie was brought in and put on a side table, and I made a hearty supper, for I was as hungry as a hawk, while Mr Dance was complimented and at last dismissed.

"And now, squire," said the doctor.

"And now, Livesey," said the squire in the same breath.

"One at a time, one at a time," laughed Dr Livesey. "You have heard of this Flint, I suppose?"

"Heard of him!" cried the squire. "Heard of him, you say! He was the blood thirstiest buccaneer that sailed. Blackbeard was a child to Flint. The Spaniards were so afraid of him that, I tell you, sir, I was sometimes proud he was an Englishman. I've seen his topsails with these eyes, off Trinidad, and the cowardly son of a rum puncheon that I sailed with retreated—retreated, sir, into Port of Spain."

"Well, I've heard of him myself, in England," said the doctor. "But the point is, had he money?"

"Money!" cried the squire. "Have you heard the story? What were

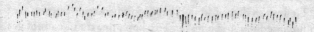

these villains after but money? What do they care for but money? For what would they risk their rascal carcasses but money?"

"That we shall soon know," replied the doctor. "But you are so confoundedly hot-headed and exclamatory that I cannot get a word in. What I want to know is this: Supposing that I have here in my pocket some clue to where Flint buried his treasure, will that treasure amount to much?"

"Amount, sir!" cried the squire. "It will amount to this: If we have the clue you talk about, I'll fit out a ship in Bristol dock, and take you and Hawkins along, and I'll have that treasure if I search a year."

"Very well," said the doctor. "Now, then, if Jim is agreeable, we'll open the packet," and he laid it before him on the table.

The bundle was sewn together, and the doctor had to get out his instrument case and cut the stitches with his medical scissors. It contained two things—a book and a sealed paper.

"First of all we'll try the book," observed the doctor.

The squire and I were both peering over his shoulder as he opened it, for Dr Livesey had kindly motioned me to come round from the side table, where I had been eating, to enjoy the sport of the search. On the first page there were only some scraps of writing, such as a man with a pen in his hand might make for idleness or practice. One was the same as the tattoo mark, "Billy Bones his fancy"; then there was "Mr W. Bones, mate", "No more rum", "Off Palm Key he got itt," and some other snatches, mostly single words and unintelligible. I could not help wondering who it was that had "got itt," and what "itt" was that he got. A knife in his back as like as not.

"Not much instruction there," said Dr Livesey as he passed on. The next ten or twelve pages were filled with a curious se

ries of entries. There was a date at one end of the line and at the other a sum of money, as in common account books, but instead of explanatory writing, only a varying number of crosses between the two. On the 12th of June, 1745, for instance, a sum of seventy pounds had plainly become due to someone, and there was nothing but six crosses to explain the cause. In a few cases, to be sure, the name of a place would be added, as "Offe Caraccas"; or a mere entry of latitude and longitude, as "62° 17' 20", 19° 2' 40"."

The record lasted over nearly twenty years, the amount of the separate entries growing larger as time went on, and at the end a grand total had been made out after five or six wrong additions, and these words appended, "Bones, his pile."

"I can't make head or tail of this," said Dr Livesey.

"The thing is as clear as noonday," cried the squire. "This is the black-hearted hound's account book. These crosses stand for the names of ships or towns that they sank or plundered. The sums are the scoundrel's share, and where he feared the location wasn't clear, you see he added something clearer. 'Offe Caraccas,' now; you see, here was some unhappy vessel boarded off that coast. God help the poor souls that manned her—coral long ago."

"Right!" said the doctor. "See what it is to be a traveller. Right! And the amounts increase, you see, as he rose in rank."

There was little else in the volume but a few bearings of places noted in the blank leaves towards the end and a table for reducing French, English, and Spanish moneys to a common value.

"Thrifty man!" cried the doctor. "He wasn't the one to be cheated."

"And now," said the squire, "for the other."

The paper had been sealed in several places with a thimble by way of seal; the very thimble, perhaps, that I had found in the captain's pocket. The doctor opened the seals with great care, and there fell out the map of an island, with latitude and longitude, soundings, names of hills and bays and inlets, and every particular that would be needed to bring a ship to a safe anchorage upon its shores. It was about nine miles long and five across, shaped, you might say, like a fat dragon standing up, and had two fine landlocked harbours, and a hill in the centre part marked "The Spyglass." There were several additions of a later date, but above all, three crosses of red ink—two on the north part of the island, one in the southwest—and beside this last, in the same red ink, and in a small, neat hand, very different from the captain's tottery characters, these words: "Bulk of treasure here."

Over on the back the same hand had written this further information:

Tall tree, Spyglass shoulder, bearing a point to the N. of N.N.E.

Skeleton Island E.S.E. and by E.

Ten feet.

The bar silver is in the north cache; you can find it by the trend of the east hummock, ten fathoms south of the black crag with the face on it.

The arms are easy found, in the sand hill, N. point of north inlet cape, bearing E. and a quarter N.

J.F.

That was all; but brief as it was, and to me incomprehensible, it filled the squire and Dr Livesey with delight.

"Doctor," said the squire, "you will give up your practice at

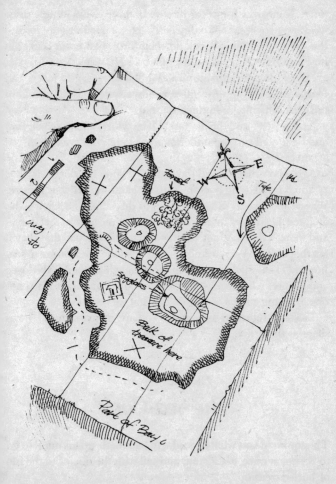

once. Tomorrow I start for Bristol. In three weeks' time—three weeks!—two weeks—ten days—we'll have the best ship, sir, and the choicest crew in England. Hawkins shall come as cabin boy. You'll make a splendid cabin boy, Hawkins. You, Livesey, are ship's doctor; I am admiral. We'll take Redruth, Joyce, and Hunter. We'll have favourable winds, a quick passage, and not the least difficulty in finding the spot."

"Trelawney," said the doctor, "I'll go with you and so will Jim, and be a credit to the undertaking. There's only one man I'm afraid of."

"And who's that?" cried the squire. "Name the dog, sir!"

"You," replied the doctor, "for you cannot hold your tongue. We are not the only men who know of this map. The fellows who attacked the inn tonight and the rest who stayed aboard that ship—and more, I dare say, not far off—are all determined that they'll get that money. We must none of us be alone until we get to sea. Jim and I shall stick together in the meanwhile. You'll take Joyce and Hunter when you ride to Bristol, and from first to last, not one of us must breathe a word of what we've found."

"Livesey," returned the squire, "you are always right. I'll be as silent as the grave."

Chapter Seven
The Sea-Cook

The squire meant what he said. He had made up his mind to go to Bristol at once, get a crew, and sail with the doctor to the isle of buried treasure.

The next day the squire went to Bristol, and the doctor went to London on business of his own. It was longer than the squire had thought before they were ready to go to sea. Days and weeks passed. For safety I lived at the Hall in charge of Redruth, a servant of the squire's who was to sail with us.

One morning a letter came from the squire. All was ready, it said, and the doctor and I were to join him at Bristol as soon as possible. He had bought a ship—a fine schooner named *Hispaniola*—and had been greatly helped in getting a crew by an old one-legged sea-cook, known as Long John Silver.

It was all like an exciting dream when Tom Redruth and I reached Bristol. We walked along the quays and beside the ships that were moored there. In one, sailors were singing at their work; and in another there were men high over my head, hanging by threads that seemed no thicker than a spider's. Though I had lived by the shore all my life, I seemed never to have been near the sea till then. The smell of tar and salt was something new. I saw many old sailors, with rings in their ears, and whiskers curled in ringlets, and tarry pigtails, and their swaggering, clumsy sea-walk.

If I had seen as many kings I could not have been more delighted.

And I was going to sea myself; to sea in a schooner, with a piping boatswain, and pigtailed singing seamen; to sea, bound for an unknown island, and to seek for buried treasure!

After breakfast on my first day in the town, the squire sent me with a note to John Silver, who kept an inn called the "Spyglass". I should easily find the place, he said, by following the line of the docks, and keeping a sharp lookout for a little tavern with a large brass telescope for a sign. I set off, glad to have this

chance to see more of the ships and seamen, and picked my way among a great crowd of people and carts and bales until I found the tavern in question.

It was a bright little place. The sign was newly painted; the windows had neat red curtains; the floor was cleanly sanded. It seemed filled by a crowd of sailor-men. They talked so loudly that I hung at the door, almost afraid to enter.

As I was waiting, a man came out of a side room. I was sure he must be Long John. His left leg was cut off close by the hip, and under the left shoulder he carried a crutch, hopping about on it like a bird. He seemed in the most cheerful spirits, whistling as he moved about among the tables, with a merry word or a slap on the shoulder for the more favoured of his guests.

When he found I was to be cabin-boy of the *Hispaniola*, he shook hands and said he was glad to see me.

Then a startling thing happened.

One of the men in the inn suddenly got up and made a dive for the door. I saw his face. My heart gave a leap.

"Stop him!" I cried. "It's Black Dog!"

"I don't care twopence who he is," cried Silver, "but he's gone without paying for his drink. Harry, run and catch him."

A man near the door ran off after Black Dog, but presently came back out of breath and said that Black Dog had run too fast and escaped him.

"Jim, my lad," said Silver, "we'd better go and tell the squire all about this. I'll put on my old cocked hat and step along with you.... "

We walked to the ship where I saw, for the first time, Captain Smollett, sailing-master of the *Hispaniola*. He was a stern sort of man, and I soon saw that the squire didn't like him very much.

Almost as soon as I was on board and in the cabin, he came to make a complaint, having first sent a message asking to speak to the squire and Dr Livesey.

"Well, Captain Smollett," asked Mr Trelawney, when the seaman was shown in, "what have you to say?"

"Sir," he said stiffly to the squire, "I will speak plain to you. I don't like this voyage—and I don't like the men."

"Perhaps, sir, you don't like your employer?" said the squire angrily. "Perhaps you don't like the ship, or the— "

Dr Livesey broke in, saying: "Wait a moment. Why, Captain, don't you like this voyage?"

"I was engaged on sealed orders—I don't know where we're going, or why we're going there. Or, rather, I *didn't* know. *Now*, I've heard a thing or two. I find that every member of the crew knows more than I do. I don't call that fair, now, do you?"

"No," said Dr Livesey thoughtfully, "I don't."

"Next," said the captain, "I learn we are going after treasure—hear it from my own men, mind you. I don't like treasure voyages when they are secret, and the secret has been told to everybody."

Dr Livesey nodded.

"And what's wrong with the crew?" he asked. "Are they not good seamen?"

"I don't like them, sir," returned Captain Smollett, "and I think I should have chosen them myself."

"Perhaps you should," the doctor agreed. "Well, now, captain, tell us what you want."

"Very good," said the captain. "You gentlemen are determined to go on this voyage, which may prove more dangerous than you think. Well, I suggest that the guns and gunpowder should be stored here in the cabin instead of in the forehold; and also

that the men of your own whom you are bringing should be given berths nearer your own."

"Anything else?" asked the doctor.

"There's been too much blabbing. I hear talk of the map of an island, with crosses on it to show where treasure is; and that the island lies—"

And he named the position of the island exactly.

"I never told anyone that!" cried the squire.

"The men know it, sir," returned the captain shortly.

The doctor and I knew that the squire was a great talker, but I felt sure that not even he would have talked about the map.

In the end it was agreed to do as Captain Smollett had suggested.

We were all hard at work moving the guns when the last man or two of the crew, and Long John with them, came aboard from a shore-boat. The cook came up the side as nimbly as a monkey, and as soon as he saw what was being done, he shouted: "So ho, mates, what's this?"

"We're moving the guns and powder, John," answered one of the men.

"Why, we'll miss the morning tide if we do," cried Long John.

"My orders," said the captain shortly. "Go below, my man. The crew will want supper."

"Aye, aye, sir!" answered the cook, and, touching his forelock, he disappeared in the direction of the galley.

"That's a good man, captain," said the doctor.

"Very likely, sir," returned Captain Smollett shortly. Then he turned to me and said: "Here, ship's boy, off with you to the cook and get some work. You'll be treated the same as the rest."

I didn't think I was going to like Captain Smollett.

All that night we were in a great bustle getting things stowed in their place. I was dog-tired when, a little before dawn, the crew began to man the capstan-bars. Nothing would have made me leave the deck, however; all was so new and interesting to me— the shouted commands, the shrill note of the whistle, the men bustling to their places in the glimmer of the ship's lanterns.

"Now, Long John, give us a song," cried one voice.

"The old one," cried another.

"Ay, ay, mates," said Long John, who was standing by, with his crutch under his arm, and at once broke out in the words I knew so well:

"Fifteen men on the dead man's chest"—

and then the whole crew joined in the chorus—

"Yo-ho-ho, and a bottle of rum!"

In that exciting moment it carried me back to the old "Admiral Benbow" in a second; and I seemed to hear the voice of the captain piping in the chorus....

Soon the anchor was up and hanging dripping in the bows. The sails began to fill and the land and shipping flitted by on either side.

The *Hispaniola* had at last begun her voyage to the Isle of Treasure.

Chapter Eight
The Apple Barrel

I shall not describe in detail all the events of our voyage. Before we came to Treasure Island, however, there happened two or

three things of which you should hear. The first was something of a mystery....

One dark night, when the sea was running high, we lost the mate, whose name was Arrow. He must have gone over the side, though no one could tell when or how the thing had happened. The captain thought him little loss, for he drank too much— though, there again, we could never make out where he got the drink. He had shown himself to be useless as an officer, and had small control over the men.

On the other hand, the coxswain, Israel Hands, was a fine seaman, and a great friend of Long John Silver's. As for the cook, he was a wonder. The crew respected and even obeyed him, and the way he skipped about on his wooden leg was astonishing. He was always kind to me; he kept the galley, where he cooked, as clean as a new pin; the dishes were hung up in rows, and his parrot, which he called Captain Flint, was in a cage in one corner.

A strange bird, that parrot. It would say, "Pieces of eight! Pieces of eight!" over and over again at such a pace that you would wonder it was not out of breath. I knew that "pieces of eight" meant gold coins, and it seemed a funny thing for a bird to say.

John Silver said it might well be a hundred years old, and that it had sailed with some of the most famous pirates and seen more wickedness than any bird alive. When he gave it sugar from his pocket it would swear and swear, using the most terrible language I ever heard, until John threw his handkerchief over the cage.

Meanwhile the squire and the captain were still not the best of friends. The captain never spoke but when he was spoken to, and then sharp and short and dry, and not a word wasted. He said that the *Hispaniola* was a good ship, but he still didn't like

the voyage or the crew, who were being spoiled by the squire's generosity.

There was some truth in this. There was extra rum to drink if the squire heard that one of the men had a birthday—which seemed to happen pretty often—and a barrel of apples stood where any man could take one if he had the fancy.

The captain thought that apple barrel just nonsense. I heard him say to Dr Livesey: "No good will come of spoiling these men. You mark my words."

Good did come of the apple barrel, however, as you shall hear. I would go so far as to say it saved the lives of some of us.

This is how it came about.

We knew, from our charts, that we were nearing the island. The weather was fine and the sea quiet. We had a steady breeze abeam and the *Hispaniola* rolled steadily.

Now, just after sundown, when all my work was over, I thought I should like an apple. I ran on deck. The watch was all forward looking out for the island. The man at the helm was whistling away gently to himself, and that was the only sound except the swish of the sea against the bows and around the sides of the ship.

The apple barrel was nearly empty and I had to get right into it to reach one from the bottom. I was about to climb out when somebody came and leaned against it and began to talk to another man. It was Long John Silver's voice I heard, and his first words made me stay still in the barrel, suddenly wide-eyed and fearful.

"Flint was our captain in those days," he said. "I was quarter-master of the ship. In the same fight that I lost my leg, old

Pew lost his eyes. Lad, I tell you I've seen Flint's ship red with blood and fit to sink with her weight of gold."

"Ah!" cried another voice, full of admiration, "he was a great man, was Flint."

The voice was that of the youngest hand on board. His name was Dick. Silver went on to tell him of the riches a man might win from piracy, if he had the sense not to waste all he gained. He said that he had his own money safely tucked away in different places, and how even Flint himself was afraid of him, and that anybody who sailed under him would be sure to do well.

"Well, I didn't like the job till I had this talk with you, John," said the lad, "but I'll shake hands on it now."

"And a brave lad you are," answered Silver, shaking hands so heartily that all the barrel shook, "and smart, too. A finer gentleman of fortune I never set eyes on."

I understood well enough what all this must mean; "a gentleman of fortune" was just a fancy name for a pirate, and John Silver was planning to get this young man into his power.

I heard Silver give a little whistle. Another man strolled up, and when he spoke I knew it was Israel Hands, the coxswain.

" Dick's with us," said Silver. "He's smart."

"Oh, I know'd Dick was all right," said Hands smoothly. "He's no fool, is Dick. But look here," he went on, "what I want to know is, how long are we going to wait? I've had just about enough of Cap'n Smollett. He's ordered me about long enough, by thunder! I want to go into that cabin, I do. I want their pickles and wines, and that."

"Israel," said Silver, "your head ain't much good, and never was. But at least you're able to hear—because your ears are

big enough. Now, here's what I say: you'll keep your berth forward, and you'll live hard, and you'll speak soft, and you'll keep off the drink, till I give the word. Have you got that, my son?"

"Well, I don't say no, do I?" grumbled Hands. "What I say is, when? That's what I say."

"When! By the holy powers!" cried Silver. "I'll tell you when. The last moment I can manage—and that's when. Here's Cap'n Smollett sails the blessed ship for us. Here's this squire and doctor with a map and such. Well, I mean this squire and doctor to find Flint's treasure, and help us to get it aboard, by the powers. Then we'll see. If I was sure of you all I'd have Cap'n Smollett take us halfway home again before I struck. I've seen a thing or two at sea, I have, and many's the brave lad that's been hanged all for this hurry, hurry, hurry."

"But," asked Dick, "what are we going to do with 'em after we have struck?"

"There's the man for me!" said Silver. "That's what I call business. Well, mates, I give my vote—death for the lot of 'em! When I'm in Parliament and riding in my coach, I don't want any of them coming home to blab. Wait is what I say; but when the time comes, why, finish them off! One thing I claim—I claim Trelawney. I'll tear his head off with these hands. . . . Dick," he added, "you just jump up and get me an apple out of the barrel."

You may guess the terror I was in! I should have leaped out and run for it, if I had found the strength. I heard Dick begin to rise, and then the voice of Hands saying:

"You don't want an apple, John! Let's have a go at the rum."

So they sent off Dick for the spirits, and when he returned

each drank to Silver's toast: "Here's to ourselves, and hold your luff, plenty of prizes and plenty of duff."

Just then a sort of brightness fell upon me in the barrel, and, looking up, I found the moon had risen and was shining white on the sails. Almost at the same time the voice of the lookout shouted:

"Land-ho!"

Chapter Nine
The Island

There was a great rush of feet across the deck. I could hear people tumbling up from the cabin and the forecastle. In the bustle and excitement that followed I slipped out of the barrel and joined the shouting crowd on the open deck.

I looked forward over the rail. Away to the south-west, clear in the moonlight, I saw two low hills about a couple of miles apart, and rising behind one of them a third and higher hill, with a peak as sharp as a cone.

There, at last, was Treasure Island, with its three pointed hills.

So much I saw, almost in a dream, for I had not yet got over my horrid fear of a minute or two before. Then I heard the voice of Captain Smollett, shouting his orders. The *Hispaniola* was laid a couple of points nearer the wind, and now sailed a course that would just clear the island on the east.

"Well, men," the captain shouted, "has any of you ever seen that land before?" "I have, sir," cried Silver. "I watered there with a ship I was cook in."

"The anchorage is on the south, behind an islet, isn't it?"

"Yes, sir. It's called Skeleton Island. It was a great place for pirates once, and we had a man on board who knew all their names for it. That hill to the north they call the Fore-mast Hill. The big 'un, with the cloud on it, they used to call the Spyglass, because of a look-out they kept there."

I remembered, as he spoke these last words, that Long John's own little tavern on the docks at Bristol was named "The Spyglass".

"I have a chart here," said Captain Smollett. "See if that's the place."

Long John's eyes burned in his head as he took the chart, but I knew by the fresh look of the paper that it was not the one I had found in the captain's chest. It was a copy, without the red crosses and the written notes. Silver must have been very disappointed, but had the strength of mind to hide it.

"Yes, sir," he said, "this is the spot all right—and very prettily drawn out." He went on to speak of currents and anchorages. "Right you was, sir," he finished, "to haul your wind and keep the weather of the island. Leastways, if you was meaning to drop anchor and careen, there's no better place for that in these waters."

"Thank you, my man," said the captain. "I'll ask you, later on, to give us your help. You may go."

I was surprised at the cool way Long John showed how well he knew the island. And I own I was half-frightened when I saw him come smiling towards me. He did not know that I had overheard him from the apple barrel, but I could scarcely hide a shudder when he laid his hand upon my arm.

"Ah," he said, "this island is a sweet spot, Jim. What a time

you'll have! You'll bathe, and you'll climb trees, and you'll hunt goats. You'll get aloft on them hills like a goat yourself. Why, it makes me young again, to think of it. When you want to do a bit of exploring, you just ask old John and he'll give you some food to take along."

And with the friendliest slap on the shoulder, he hobbled off and went below.

Captain Smollett, the squire, and Dr Livesey were talking together on the quarter-deck, and, anxious as I was to tell them my story, I dared not interrupt them openly. Then, as luck would have it, Dr Livesey called me to his side.

"Jim," he said, "run down to the cabin and bring up my pipe, there's a good lad."

"Doctor," I said softly, "let me speak. Get the captain and the squire down to the cabin, and then make some pretence to send for me. I have terrible news."

I saw his face change a little, but he gave no other sign.

"Thank you, Jim," he said, quite loudly, "that was all I wanted to know," as if he had asked me a question.

With that he turned on his heel and rejoined the other two. They spoke together for a little, and the next thing I heard was the captain giving an order, and all hands were piped on deck.

"My lads," said Captain Smollett, "I've a word to say to you. This land that we have sighted is the place we have been sailing to. Mr Trelawney and the doctor and I are going below to the cabin to drink your health and luck, and you'll have rum served out for you to drink our health and luck."

The cheer that followed rang out so full and hearty that I could hardly believe these same men were plotting for our blood.

"One more cheer for Cap'n Smollett," cried Long John, when the first had died away.

And this also was given with a will.

The three gentlemen went below, and not long after word was sent that Jim Hawkins was wanted in the cabin.

I found the three of them seated round the table, with a bottle of wine before them. The stern window was open, for it was a warm night, and you could see the moon shining behind on the ship's wake.

"Now, Hawkins," said the squire, "you have something to say. Speak up."

I told them all that I had heard, while they listened in silence. Not one of them made so much as a movement, and they kept their eyes on my face from first to last.

"Jim," said Dr Livesey, "take a seat."

They made me sit down at table beside them, poured me out a glass of wine, and all three, and each with a bow, drank my good health, for my luck and courage.

"Now, captain," said the squire, "you were right, and I was wrong. I own myself an ass and I await your orders."

"No more an ass than I, sir," replied the captain. "I should have smelt all this out. I never heard of a crew that meant to mutiny without showing signs of it beforehand, but this crew beats me," he added, shaking his head.

"Captain," said the doctor. "it's all Silver's doing. He's a very remarkable man."

"He'd look remarkably well hanging from a yard-arm, sir," said Captain Smollett grimly. "But this talk doesn't lead to anything. I see three or four points, and, with Mr Trelawney's permission, I'll name them."

"You, sir, are the captain. It's for you to speak," said the squire grandly.

"First point," began Mr Smollett, "we must go on, because we can't turn back. If I gave the word to go about, they would rise at once. Second point, we have time before us, until this treasure's found. Third point, some of the hands are faithful. Now, it's got to come to blows sooner or later, and I suggest that we start the fight when they least expect it. We can depend, I take it, on your home servants, Mr Trelawney?"

"As upon myself," declared the squire.

"Three of them," reckoned the captain, "and ourselves make seven. Now, about the honest hands?"

"Most likely the men Trelawney picked up for himself, without Silver to help him," said the doctor.

"Well, gentlemen," said the captain, "the best that I can say is not much. We must keep a sharp look-out."

"Jim, here," said the doctor, "can help us more than anyone. The men are not shy of him, and Jim keeps his eyes and ears open."

"Hawkins, I have great faith in you," added the squire.

I felt pretty helpless, and yet in the end it was through me that we were saved. In the meantime, things looked bad; there were only seven of the crew of twenty-six on whom we could rely, and one of them was a boy—myself. The grown men on our side were six to their nineteen....

Next morning we were close to the island and could see it very clearly. Grey-coloured woods covered a large part of it. There were streaks of yellow sand along the shore, and the hills ran up in spires of naked rock.

The *Hispaniola* was rolling in a heavy swell. I had to cling to

ropes in order to keep my feet. The whole ship was creaking, groaning and jumping, and when it rolled like that I always felt unwell in my stomach. Perhaps it was this that made me hate the thought of Treasure Island, with its grey woods and rocky hills and the high sea thundering on its steep, yellow beaches.

In spite of the heavy swell, there was no wind, and the boats had to go out to tow the ship around the corner of the island. I went with one of them, though I had no business there. The heat was sweltering and the men grumbled fiercely over their work. Job Anderson, the boatswain, was in charge of my boat, and instead of keeping the crew in order he grumbled as loud as the worst.

"Well," he said, with an oath, "it's not forever."

I thought this was a bad sign. The men, up to that day, had worked briskly and with a will; but a change had come over them at the very sight of the island.

Long John, who knew the coast, stood by the steersman and conned the ship. He seemed to know the passage like the palm of his hand.

At last we dropped anchor in a narrow arm of the sea, where trees came down almost to the water's edge. The bottom was clean sand. The plunge of our anchor sent up clouds of birds wheeling and crying over the woods; but in less than a minute they were down again, and all was once more silent.

There was no sign of life on shore. We might have been the first that had ever anchored there since the island arose out of the seas.

There was not a breath of air moving. I saw that there were swamps among the woods, and the trees had a kind of poison-

ous greenness. The air held the smell of dead leaves and rotting logs. I noticed the doctor sniffing and sniffing, like someone tasting a bad egg.

"I don't know about treasure," I heard him say, "but I'm sure there's fever here."

On board the ship the men just lay about the decks, growling and muttering together.

Mutiny, it was clear, hung over us like a thunder cloud. The slightest order was received by a black look, and grudgingly and carelessly obeyed. Long John saw it plainly enough, and he did his level best to get everybody back into a good temper. He was all smiles to everyone. He didn't want his plot spoiled by starting too soon!

We had another talk in the cabin. The captain said that if he gave any more orders trouble would start at once. Silver was the only man who could keep the crew in order.

"What I propose is to give the men an afternoon ashore," he said. "If they go, then we'll seize the ship and stop them coming back. If none go, we'll hold the cabin, and defend it as best we can. If some go, Silver will bring them back as quiet as mice."

It was decided. Loaded pistols were handed out to the men we could trust; we told Hunter, Joyce, and Redruth—the squire's own servants—what the trouble was. Then the captain went on deck to tell the men that they could go ashore, and that he'd fire a gun an hour before sundown, as a signal for them to return.

The men gave a cheer as if they expected to fall over the treasure as soon as they were on shore. The captain went below and left them to arrange things just as they wanted.

At last the party was ready; six were to stay on board, and the remaining thirteen, including Silver, were to go ashore. At the last minute I decided to go with them. I slipped over the side and curled up in the foresheets of the nearest boat just before she was shoved off.

No one took notice of me, only the bow oarsman saying, "Is that you, Jim? Keep your head down."

Silver, from the other boat, looked sharply over and called to know if that were me; and from that moment I began to regret what I had done.

The crews raced for the beach, but the boat I was in had a good start and touched the shore first. In a moment I had caught a branch, swung myself out, and plunged into the nearest thicket.

I heard Silver give a shout: "Jim, come back! Jim, Jim!"

I paid no heed. I went jumping and ducking and breaking through the undergrowth, running straight before my nose till I could run no longer.

Chapter Ten
The First Blow

I was so pleased at having given the slip to Long John, that I began to enjoy myself and look around me at the strange land I was in, with its swamps and strange trees, and the hills shining in the sun above them.

All at once a great cloud of birds flew up, and hung screaming and circling above the woods. I guessed that some of the crew

must be drawing near, and soon I heard voices. These voices grew steadily louder and nearer. This made me very fearful and I crouched down behind a bush and hid there as silent as a mouse.

There were two men talking. One voice I recognized as Silver's, and it ran on for a long while with few interruptions from the other. At last the voices grew quieter and the birds wheeled down to their trees.

I now began to feel that it was my duty to find out as much as I could, so I crept silently towards the sound of the voices. At last I could lift my head and see, through the leaves, two men standing in a little green dell. The sun was beating down on them, but Silver had thrown his hat upon the ground. He looked angry.

"Tom," I heard him say, "are you coming in with us or not? It's the only way you can save your neck, I'll tell you that."

"Silver," said the other, and his voice shook, "I thought you were an honest man. Will you let yourself be led astray by a bunch of thieves? I'd sooner lose my hand! If I turn against my captain—"

All of a sudden he was interrupted by a noise. Far away among the woods there arose a sound like the cry of anger; and then one horrid, longdrawn scream. The rocks of the hills re-echoed it and set all the birds rising with a whirr of wings.

Tom jumped and paled at the sound, but Silver did not wink an eye. He stood where he was, resting lightly on his crutch, watching the other like a snake about to spring.

"What was that?" cried Tom.

"That?" answered Silver, and he showed his teeth in a smile. "That? Oh, I reckon that'll be Alan."

"Alan!" cried Tom, angrily. "You've killed Alan, have you? Well, he's died like a true sailor. As for you, John Silver, you're no longer any mate of mine. Kill me, too, if you can. I'll not join you, or those other murdering wretches."

With that he turned his back on Silver and walked off towards the beach. But he did not get far. With a cry, John Silver seized the branch of a tree, whipped the crutch out of his arm-pit, and hurled it like a spear. It struck poor Tom right between the shoulders in the middle of his back. His hand flew up, he gave a sort of gasp, and fell.

Before he could rise Silver gave two long bounds and was on top of him. I saw a knife flash in the sunlight, as Silver twice buried it up to the hilt in poor Tom's back.

The whole world swam before me in a whirling mist. When I came again to myself, Silver was wiping his blood-stained knife upon a wisp of grass. Then he got once more to his feet, his crutch under his arm, his hat upon his head, brought out a whistle from his pocket, and blew three loud blasts that rang far across the heated air.

I did not know the meaning of this signal, but it instantly awoke my fears. More men would be coming. I might be found. They had already killed two honest men. It might be my turn next.

I began to crawl back again, as quickly and silently as I could. As I did so, I heard shouts coming and going between Silver and his friends. These sounds lent me wings. As soon as I thought that they would not see or hear me, I ran as I had never ran before, not caring where I went as long as I was moving away from the murderers. As I ran, the fear grew and grew upon me, until I was in a kind of frenzy.

Could anyone be more lost than I! When that gun was fired from the ship to recall all hands, I wouldn't dare go down to the boats among those men whom I now knew to be murderers and cut-throats. To me, then, it seemed more than likely that one of them would wring my neck like a snipe's. It was likely that my absence itself would be evidence to them of my alarm, and therefore of my knowledge of their mutiny.

It was all over, I thought. Goodbye to the *Hispaniola!* Goodbye to the doctor, the squire, and the captain! There was nothing left for me but starvation, or death at the hands of the mutineers.

While I thought all this, I had kept running without really seeing where I went. A quick glance showed me that I had drawn near to the foot of the little hill with the two peaks, which had tall trees growing upon the lower slopes.

As I looked among those trees a sound brought me to a standstill with a thumping heart. A shower of stones came rattling and bumping down the side of the hill. I swung round and was in time to see a shape leap swiftly behind the trunk of a tree.

Chapter Eleven

The Man of the Island

I felt a chill crawl up my spine. I felt that eyes were watching me, waiting to see what I would do next. I hesitated, and was filled with terror. What was this creature of the woods? I thought of

cannibals and almost cried for help, but my fear of Silver kept me quiet.

I was now, it seemed, cut off on both sides and surrounded by danger. Behind me were the murderers, and in front of me was this lurking, sinister shape. I decided that I preferred the dangers that I knew to the unknown threat ahead. I turned sharply on my heel and began to make my way back towards the shore.

After a few steps, I swung round. I was in time to see the creature flitting from trunk to trunk. My heart gave a big hop. The creature was running on two legs, though stooped almost double as it ran. It seemed dark and shaggy, but I knew that it was a man of sorts.

I halted and something of my courage came back. I remembered that I had a loaded pistol stuck in my belt. I took its butt in my hand and began to walk towards this man of the island. He must have been watching me closely. As soon as I made a move, he came out from behind a tree and took a step to meet me. I walked on. He stopped, drew back, came forward again, and then, to my amazement, he threw himself on his knees and held out his hands to me.

I stopped.

"Who are you?" I asked, and my voice sounded odd in my ears.

"Ben Gunn," he answered, and his voice sounded like a rusty lock. "I'm poor Ben Gunn, and I haven't spoken to another man these three years past."

I saw now that he was a white man, though his skin was burned dark by the sun. Even his lips were black, and his blue eyes looked quite startling in so dark a face. His clothes were just bits and tatters of rag, pieces of old ship's sail held together by sticks and

bones. About his waist, however, he wore an old, brass-buckled, leather belt.

I started at his words.

"Three years?" I cried. "Were you shipwrecked?"

"No, mate," he answered sadly. "I was marooned."

I knew what he meant. I had often heard that pirates would sometimes choose to punish a man by putting him ashore on a lonely island with a little powder and shot, and there leave him to fend for himself. I looked in awe at this poor creature with his great mane of matted hair and his long shaggy beard.

I no longer felt any fear of him at all.

"Three years," he said again, "and all that time I've lived on goats, and berries, and oysters. But, mate, I'd love a bit of *real* food. You don't happen to have a piece of cheese about you, do you? No? Well, many's the long night I've dreamed of eating cheese—"

"If I can get aboard the ship again," I said, "you shall have cheese by the stone."

All this time he had been feeling the cloth of my jacket, touching my hands, and looking at my boots, showing a childish pleasure at seeing another human being.

"What do you call yourself, mate?" he asked me.

"Jim," I told him.

"Well, Jim," he said, and looked all round and lowered his voice to a whisper, "I've lived a long time on this island, and I'm rich! Rich! And I'll make you rich, too, I will! You'll be glad that you were the first that found me!"

Then a shadow came over his face, and he tightened his grip on my arm and wagged a bony finger in my face, as he asked fearfully:

"Now, Jim, you tell me true: that ain't Flint's ship, is it?"

I shook my head.

"It's not Flint's ship," I said. "Flint is dead, but there are some of his old crew on board."

He started at that.

"Not a man—with one—leg?" he gasped.

"Silver?" I asked.

"That's it," he answered; "that were his name."

"He's cook on board," I said, "and the ringleader, too."

He was still holding me by the wrist, and I felt his fingers tighten.

"If he sent you, I'm as good as dead," said Ben Gunn.

It occurred to me that this poor man might be able to help us, and I told him the whole story of our voyage and the trouble in which we now found ourselves. He listened with keen interest, and when I had done he patted me on the head.

"You're a good lad, Jim," he said. "Well, you just put your trust in Ben Gunn—Ben Gunn's the man to do it. If I helped you, do you think your squire would give me a share of what's mine already, in a manner of speaking?"

I told him that he could count on the squire to give him a share in the treasure; it had been agreed that all the crew were to have a share in anything we found.

"*And* a passage home?" he added, with a worried look.

"Yes, for sure," I cried. "If we get rid of the others, we shall want you to help work the vessel home."

"Ah," he said, "so you would. Now, I'll tell you something," he went on. "I was in Flint's ship when he buried the treasure. He took six men with him to do it, but he came back alone! Dead men tell no tales, see? Well, I was in another ship three years back and we sighted this island again. 'Boys,' said I, 'here's Flint's

treasure: let's land and find it.' Well, we landed and for twelve days we looked for it, and couldn't find it, and then *they* said to me, 'As for you, Ben Gunn, you can stay here and find Flint's treasure for yourself!' And they gave me a musket, and a spade, and a pickaxe—and here they left me. Three years I've been here, Jim, and I've had lots of time to spare, I have. Now, you go to the squire and tell him that Ben Gunn is a good man, and knows a thing or two about this island."

With that he winked and pinched me hard.

"All right," I said, "I'll tell him that, but how am I to get back to the ship?"

"Ah," he said, "that's a snag, to be sure. Well, there's my boat that I made with my two hands. I keep her under the white rock. If the worst comes to the worst, we might try that after dark. Hi! What's that?" he added breathlessly.

Just then, although it was still an hour or two before sunset, all the island echoed to the thunder of a cannon.

"They've begun to fight," I cried. "Follow me!"

I took to my heels at once, with Ben Gunn trotting easily and lightly at my side, and calling out directions as we ran. After a little while the cannon-shot was followed by a volley from muskets and pistols.

Another pause, and then, not a quarter of a mile in front of me, I saw the Union Jack break out and flutter in the air above a wood.

It was both a shock and a surprise, but I'll have to let Dr Livesey tell the next bit of the story because I wasn't there to see what happened.

Chapter Twelve
Dr Livesey's Story

It was about half past one when the boats went ashore. If there had been a strong wind we should have fought the six mutineers who were still on board, and put to sea again. That, no doubt, would have been the best way to treat our mutineers, but, as luck would have it, there was a severe lack of wind; and to complete our helplessness, down came Hunter with the news that Jim Hawkins had slipped into a boat and was gone ashore with the rest.

It was a bad moment for us. We did not doubt his loyalty but we were very much alarmed for his safety. Knowing the temper that the men were in, we did not expect to see the lad alive again.

We ran on deck as soon as Hunter came down and told us that Jim had slipped into a boat and gone ashore. The heat was like a furnace blast, and the nasty smell of the place turned me sick. If ever a man smelt fever and dysentery, it was in that abominable shore where we lay anchored.

The six scoundrels who were still on board were sitting grumbling under a sail in the forecastle. Ashore we could see both the boats made fast, and a man sitting in each. One of them was whistling "Lillibullero".

Waiting was a great strain. At last we decided that Hunter and I should go ashore in a small boat to see what information we could gain. We lowered the boat, and then pulled straight in

towards the spot where a wooden fort was marked on the map that we had.

The two men who were guarding the boats seemed a little alarmed when they saw us. The whistler broke off in the middle of a bar, and I could see the pair of them talking over what they ought to do. Had they gone and told Silver, all might have turned out differently; but they had their orders, I suppose, and decided to sit quietly where they were and go back again to "Lillibullero".

There was a slight bend in the coast, and I steered so as to put it between us. We jumped out and hurried through the trees. I had a pistol in each hand for safety.

We had not gone a hundred yards when we came upon the fort.

A spring of clear water rose almost at the top of a little hill. Round the spring had been built a strong house of logs, with loop-holes to shoot from. All round this was an open space, and then a strong fence, six feet high and without any door or opening. With luck the place could be held against a small army. The best part of it was the spring, particularly as we had no supply of water on board the ship.

I was thinking things over, when we heard the cry of a man at the point of death. I remember how it made my pulse go dot and carry one. "Jim Hawkins has been killed," was my first thought.

I have been a soldier as well as a doctor. I decided at once that the best thing we could do would be to go ashore and occupy the fort. Without wasting any more time, we went back to the shore and pulled hard for the schooner.

Back on the ship I found them all as white as sheets and greatly

troubled by the cry they had heard. Captain Smollett told me that one of the six mutineers—Abraham Gray—had nearly fainted when he heard it, and we had hopes that he might be persuaded to join us.

We made our plans and got busy. Hunter brought the boat under the stern of the ship, and Joyce and I began loading her with powder, muskets, bags of biscuits, salted meat, a cask of brandy, and my medicine chest.

In the meantime, the squire and the captain had shouted for the coxwain, Israel Hands, who was the chief man aboard. He came on deck.

"Mr Hands," said the captain, "here are two of us and we have two pistols each. If any one of you makes a signal to the shore, that man is dead."

For the moment, this threat was enough.

When we had finished loading the boat I rowed to the shore with Joyce and Hunter and we carried our stores to the fort. Then, leaving the two men on guard, I rowed back to the ship again. We loaded the boat once more. Pork, powder, and biscuit was the cargo, with only a musket and a cutlass apiece for the squire and me and Redruth and the captain. The rest of the rams and the powder we dropped overboard in two fathoms and a half of water, so that we could see the bright steel shining far below us in the sun, on the clean sandy bottom.

By this time we could hear voices shouting in the direction of the two boats already ashore. It warned us that it was time we were off.

Redruth and the squire dropped down into the boat, and we waited for Captain Smollett. He called down to the men in the forecastle.

"Now, men, do you hear me?"

There was no answer.

"It's to you, Abraham Gray—it's to you I'm speaking."

Still no reply.

"Gray," said the captain, a little louder, "I'm leaving this ship, and I order you to follow me. I know you're a good man at heart. I give you thirty seconds to join me."

There was a pause, then a scuffle, a sound of blows, and out rushed Abraham Gray with a knife-cut on the side of the cheek. He came running to the captain, like a dog to the whistle.

"I'm with you, sir," he said.

The next moment he and the captain had dropped aboard us, and we had shoved off and were pulling for the shore.

The boat, of course, was greatly overloaded. Several times we shipped a little water, and my breeches and the tails of my coat were all soaking wet before we had gone a hundred yards. We were almost afraid to breathe, and, to make matters worse, the tide had turned and now began to carry us off our course.

Suddenly I heard the captain shout.

"The gun! Look at the ship!"

We had forgotten the ship's cannon. There, to our horror, were five of the wretches we had left behind, stripping off her tarpaulin cover. Not only that, but it flashed into my mind that the round shot and the powder for the gun had all been left behind.

"Israel Hands was Flint's gunner," said Gray hoarsely.

I could see Hands, the brandy-faced rascal, plumping down a round-shot on the deck.

"Who's the best shot among us?" asked the captain.

"The squire, without doubt," I answered.

"Mr Trelawney," said the captain calmly, please shoot Israel Hands for me."

Trelawney was as cool as steel. He raised his gun.

"Stand by," said the captain, and we stopped rowing.

The mutineers, by this time, had the gun slewed round upon its swivel, and Hands was at the muzzle with the rammer. However, we had no luck. Just as Trelawney fired, Hands stooped down, and it was one of the others who fell.

The cry he gave was echoed by voices from the shore. I saw the other pirates trooping out from among the trees and tumbling into their places in the boats.

"Row hard!" cried the captain. "We must get to the fort even if we sink the boat in doing it."

We rowed hard. We were very close in when the gun on the ship was fired. The shot must have passed over our heads, but we paid little heed to it. At that moment our over-laden boat sank under us in three feet of water, taking two of our guns with it. Mine was safe, for I held it over my head, and the captain had carried his strapped across his shoulders.

We had come to no harm, but we had no time to lose. We waded ashore as fast as we could, and as we did so we heard the cries of the mutineers coming nearer and nearer. It was clear that we would soon have to turn and fight.

We plunged into the woods. At every step we took their voices rang nearer. Soon we could hear their footfalls as they ran, and the cracking of the branches as they came tearing after us.

Another forty paces and we came to the edge of the wood. As we saw the fort in front of us seven of the mutineers came out of the trees to the south-west. They paused. In that instant the squire and I, and Hunter and Joyce from the fort, fired a scat-

tered volley. One man dropped, and the rest turned and ran back into the cover of the trees.

We raced on towards the fort.

In that same second a pistol exploded behind us. A ball whistled close past my ear, and poor Tom Redruth stumbled and fell his length on the ground. Both the squire and I returned the shot, then reloaded and turned our attention to poor Tom. I saw with half an eye that it was all over for him. We somehow managed to lift him over the fence and carried him, groaning and bleeding, into the log-house.

I examined his wound, and knew that he would soon die. The squire dropped down beside him on his knees, crying like a child.

"Be I going, doctor?" he asked.

"Tom, my man," I said, "you're going home."

"I wish I'd had a shot or two at them first," he replied. Then, after a little while of silence, he said he thought somebody might read a prayer. "It's the custom, sir," he added apologetically. Not long after, without another word, he passed away.

In the meantime, the captain and Hunter had found a long branch in the clearing outside, and had set it up at the corner of the house with the Union Jack flying from it.

When the captain came back into the loghouse, he found a second flag and covered Tom's body with it.

"All's well with him, sir," he said to the squire. "You need have no fears for a man who has been shot down doing his duty."

Just then, with a roar and a whistle, a shot from the ship's cannon passed high over the roof of the log-house and dropped far beyond us in the wood.

"Oho!" said the captain. "Blaze away! You've little enough powder already, my lads."

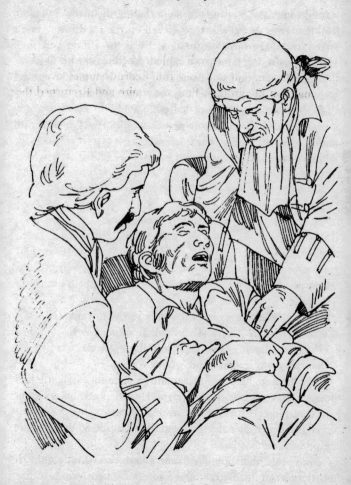

All through the evening they kept thundering away. Ball after ball flew over or fell short, or kicked up the sand in the open space round the fort. We thought it was the Union Jack they were trying to hit, but the captain refused to lower his flag.

Time passed, and I was wondering sadly what had happened to poor Jim when there came a shout from outside.

"Doctor! Squire! Captain! Are you there?"

I ran to the door and was in time to see Jim Hawkins, safe and sound, come climbing over the fence.

Now he can go on and tell his own story again.

Chapter Thirteen

The Attack

I told you how Ben Gunn and I saw the flag appear above the tree-tops.

He stopped at the sight, and caught me by the arm.

"Now." he said. "there's your friends, sure enough."

"Far more likely it's the mutineers" I answered.

Ben shook his shaggy head.

"No," he said, "if it was Silver and his men they'd fly the Jolly Roger. That's your friends, all right. Here they are ashore in the fort that Flint built years and years ago."

"Well," I said, "I must hurry on and join them. You'd better come with me."

"No, mate," said Ben, "not until I know how they would receive me. You must go on alone Jim. When you wants to find

Ben Gunn again, you know where to find him. Just where you found him today."

He was interrupted by a loud explosion, as a cannon-ball from the ship went crashing through the trees above our heads and landed in the sand not a hundred yards from where we stood talking. We both turned and ran in different directions.

For a whole hour the gun from the ship kept firing, and balls kept crashing through the woods. I moved from hiding-place to hiding-place, working my way back towards the shore. I dared not make a dash for the fort yet, because that was where the balls fell most often.

After a long time I crept down among the shore-side trees.

The sun had just set, and a cool breeze was rustling in the woods. The air, after the heat of the day, chilled me through my jacket.

I saw the *Hispaniola* with the black flag of piracy flying at her peak. Even as I looked, there came another red flash and another report that sent the echoes clattering, and one more cannon-ball whistled through the air. It was the last of the day.

A great fire was glowing among the trees, and some of the men were on the beach. From the sound of their voices I judged that they had been drinking rum. I saw, too, along the shore, the white rock where Ben Gunn had hidden his boat.

At last I turned back into the woods and moved cautiously towards the fort. I reached the fence without seeing any further sign of the pirates, and was soon warmly welcomed by my friends, who were eager to hear of my adventures.

For the rest of that evening, Captain Smollett kept us busy. Tired as we all were, two were sent out for firewood; two more were set to dig a grave for Redruth; the doctor was made cook;

and I was put sentry at the door. My eyes, I remember, kept straying to the body that lay along the wall, stiff and stark under the Union Jack.

Before supper was eaten we buried poor Tom in the sand, and stood around him for a while bareheaded in the breeze.

Late into the night we heard the mutineers roaring and singing. The doctor said grimly that, camped where they were in swampy ground, half of them would be down with fever inside a week.

I was dead tired, as you may imagine, and I slept like a log.

The rest had long been up, and had already breakfasted when I was awakened by a sudden excited shouting.

"Flag of truce," I heard someone say, and then another voice cried out:

"It's Silver himself!"

At that I jumped up, and, rubbing my eyes, ran to a loophole in the wall. I saw two men just outside the fence. One of them was waving a white cloth; the other was Long John Silver.

It was still quite early. The sky was bright and cloudless overhead, and the tops of the trees shone rosily in the sun.

"Keep indoors, men," growled the captain. "Ten to one this is a trick."

Then he shouted to the buccaneer.

"What do you want? Stand, or we fire."

"Flag of truce," cried Silver.

The captain was in the porch, keeping himself out of the way of any treacherous shot that might come. He turned and spoke to us:

"Keep a sharp look-out," he said, and then turned again to the mutineers.

"What do you want with your flag of truce?" he cried.

This time it was the other man who replied.

"Captain Silver, sir, come to make terms."

"Captain Silver!" cried Smollett. "Don't know him. Who's he?" Long John answered for himself.

"Me, sir," he said. "Since you left them these poor lads have chosen me for their captain. All I ask is your word that you'll let me away safe if I come in and talk."

"My man," answered Captain Smollett stiffly, "I have no wish to talk to you, but if you wish to talk to me, you can come, that's all. If there's any treachery, it'll be on your side."

"That's good enough, cap'n," shouted Long John cheerily.

Then he came right up to the fence, threw over his crutch, got a leg up, and dropped down on our side. He had terrible hard work to get up the slope, and his crutch kept sinking in the soft sand. At last, however, he arrived before the captain, and saluted. He was all dressed up in his best clothes; a blue coat, thick with brass buttons, hung down to his knees, and a fine laced hat was set on the back of his head.

"Here you are, my man," said the captain. "You'd better sit down."

"It's a cold morning to sit outside upon the sand," said Silver. "Ain't you going to ask me inside?"

"Why, Silver," said the captain, "if you'd been an honest man, you might have been sitting in your galley."

Silver smiled, then sat down upon the sand.

"One of you'll have to give me a hand up again, that's all," he said, and looked all round him with interest. "It's a sweet pretty place you have here," he said. "Ah, there's Jim! You're all here like a happy family."

"If you have anything to say, my man," said the captain, "you'd better say it."

"Right you are, Captain Smollett. Well, here it is. We want that treasure and we're going to have it. You hand over that chart of yours, stop shooting poor seamen—and we'll see you all safe. You do that, and I'll see you come to no harm."

Captain Smollett was lighting his pipe.

"Is that all?" he asked.

"Every last word, by thunder!" answered Silver. "Refuse that, and you've seen the last of me but my musket-balls!"

"Very good," said the captain. "Now you can hear me. If you'll come up here, one by one and with empty hands, I'll clap you all in irons, and take you to England for a fair trial. If you won't, I'll see you all at the end of a rope. You can't find the treasure. You can't sail the ship. And these are the last good words you'll get from me. I'll put a bullet in your back when next I meet you. Now get out of this, and in double quick time!"

Silver's face was a picture. His eyes were starting out of his head with anger.

"Give me a hand up! " he cried.

"Not I," answered the captain.

"Who'll give me a hand up?" he roared.

Not a man among us moved. He swore fiercely and crawled along the sand till he got hold of the porch and could hoist himself again upon his crutch. Then he spat into the spring.

"There!" he cried. "That's what I think of you. Laugh, by thunder, laugh! Before an hour's out, you'll be laughing on the other side of your faces. Them that die'll be the lucky ones."

With another dreadful oath he stumbled off, was helped over

the fence by the other man, and was soon lost to sight among the trees.

The captain looked round at us all.

"My lads," he said, "we're outnumbered, but we can beat them if we choose. Now, every man to his post!"

We expected an attack at once, but nothing happened for the moment. We waited, while the sun climbed above our girdle of trees and burned down upon the clearing. Soon the sand was baking and the log-house was like an oven. Jackets and coats were flung aside; shirts thrown open at the neck, and rolled up to the shoulders; and we stood there, each at his post, in a fever of heat and anxiety.

An hour passed away.

Then suddenly Joyce whipped up his musket and fired. His shot was answered by a volley from outside the walls. Several bullets struck the log-house, but not one of them entered; and, as the smoke cleared away and vanished, the clearing and the woods around it looked as quiet and empty as before. Not even the gleam of a musket-barrel betrayed the presence of our enemies.

There was a brief pause, and then no time for thought after that.

Suddenly, with a fierce shout, a little cloud of pirates leaped from the woods on the north side, and ran straight for the fence. At the same moment the fire was once more opened from the woods, and a rifle-ball sang through the doorway and knocked the doctor's musket into bits.

The attackers swarmed over the fence like monkeys. We fired again and again. Three men fell and lay still, but four had got over and came rushing on towards the house, shrieking and

cursing like madmen. Several shots were fired, but none seemed to have scored a hit. In a moment, the four pirates had swarmed up the slope and were upon us.

They came tumbling through the doorway. One grabbed Hunter's musket, wrenched it from his hands, and with one stunning blow stretched the poor fellow senseless upon the floor. Another one attacked the doctor with his cutlass.

The log-house was full of smoke. Cries and shouts of pain, the flashes and reports of pistol-shots, and one loud groan, rang in my ears. "Outside, lads! Fight them in the open! Cutlasses!" cried the captain.

I snatched a cutlass from the pile in the middle of the room, and dashed out of the door into the clear sunlight. Someone was close behind, but I don't know who it was. Right in front, the doctor was chasing his attacker down the hill. I saw him beat down the man's guard and then send him sprawling on his back, with a great slash across the face.

"Round the house, lads!" cried the captain urgently.

With my cutlass raised, I ran round the corner of the house. Next moment I was face to face with a pirate. He roared aloud, and his cutlass went up above his head, flashing in the sunlight. I leaped to one side, missed my footing in the soft sand, and rolled headlong down the slope.

After that things happened so swiftly that by the time I was on my feet again the fight was over, and the victory was ours. Gray, following close behind me, had cut down the man who attacked me outside the house; the doctor had wounded his assailant; another mutineer had been shot at a loophole. Of the four who had climbed the fence, only one remained on his feet—and he was now climbing back again with the fear of death upon him.

When the house had cleared of smoke we saw the price we had paid for victory. Hunter lay stunned beside his loophole. Joyce had been shot through the head and would never move again, while the captain, his face as white as death, was being held up by the squire.

The mutineers did not return—there was not so much as another shot out of the woods. Out of the eight men who had fallen in the fight, only three still breathed, and two were clearly dying. The captain was not seriously injured, but the doctor said that he must not walk or move his arm for some time to come. The pirate who had been shot at the loophole died while the doctor was dressing his wounds.

After dinner the squire and the doctor sat by the captain's side a while and talked over our position. Then, to my amazement, the doctor took up his hat and pistols, put the chart in his pocket and a musket over his shoulder, crossed the fence on the north side, and set off briskly through the trees. I guessed that he was going to meet Ben Gunn, and his departure put an idea into my own head.

It was this: I would go down to the shore, find the white rock that I had seen last evening, and make sure that Ben Gunn had hidden his boat there. I thought that we might yet find a good use for that boat.

It was lucky I had no idea of the dangers that were to follow my finding of the boat....

I was certain that I would not be allowed to leave the fort if I asked, so my plan was to slip out when nobody was watching. I picked up a couple of loaded pistols and slipped some biscuits into my pocket.

I waited, and at last I saw my chance. The squire and Gray

were busy helping the captain with his bandages. The coast was clear. I made a bolt for it over the fence, and went plunging among the trees.

Chapter Eleven
My Sea Adventure

I made my way straight for the east coast of the island. It was already late in the afternoon, although still warm and sunny. As I threaded my way through the tall woods I could hear the thunder of the surf and at last saw the sea lying blue to the far horizon.

I made my way to a point from which I could see the *Hispaniola*. She lay still in the anchorage—the only quiet water all round the island—the Jolly Roger hanging from her peak and one of the boats alongside. In it was Silver, with his parrot perched upon his shoulder, talking to two men on board. As I watched he waved and left them and began pulling in towards the shore.

The sun was going down behind the Spyglass. I knew that I must lose no time if I were to find the boat that evening. I began to work my way towards the white rock, crawling, often on all fours, among the scrub. Night had almost come when I laid my hand on its rough sides.

Right below it there was a small hollow of green turf, hidden by banks and thick brushwood; and in the centre of the hollow I found Ben Gunn's little boat. It was made of goat-skins stretched tight over a wooden frame, and was very small, even for me. Across it there lay a double paddle for rowing.

As I looked at it another idea entered my head—an idea so daring that it set my heart pounding. It was to slip out under cover of the night, cut the *Hispaniola* adrift, and let her go ashore where she fancied. Now that I had seen how the pirates left only two men on guard, I thought it might be done with little risk.

I sat down, made a meal off my biscuits, and waited for darkness. By the time the sun had gone down a heavy mist was rising from the swamps. The night would be a good one for my purpose.

When, at last, I shouldered the boat and groped my way stumblingly out of the hollow, I saw that a great fire was burning along the shore and could hear voices raised in drunken song. I carried the boat down to the water, got into it and pushed off.

It was difficult to manage and I should never have reached the ship at all but for the tide. After a little, however, I saw the *Hispaniola* take shape in the darkness.

I drew alongside and seized hold of the hawser. My heart was thumping away like mad. I could hear angry voices in the cabin; two men, it was clear, were drunk and quarrelling. On the shore behind me I could see the glow of the great camp fire, where the mutineers were gathered, shouting and singing.

I waited till the ship moved with the tide. The hawser went slack under my hand. I drew my knife and began to cut through it, one strand after another.

The moment the rope was cut the ship began to swing round. I tried to push my boat off and my hands caught a loose rope that was hanging over the side. I pulled myself up, determined to see what was happening in the cabin. Everything was quiet, and a glance within told me why the men were silent. They were fighting, locked in a deadly wrestle, each with a hand to

the other's throat. One of them I recognized as Israel Hands.

The ship gave a lurch. Her speed increased as she was caught by the tide. The men in the cabin must have guessed that something was wrong, for as I dropped back into my boat I heard a hoarse shout and then the sound of heavy feet on the stairs that led to the deck.

The boat was being swept away from the ship. All round me were little, slapping ripples.

I tried to paddle but could not hold the boat. Ever quickening, it went spinning through the narrows for the open sea. I could do nothing. I lay down in the bottom of the boat and let the sea take her. Tired as I was, I at last fell into a troubled sleep.

I awoke in the light of day to find my boat rising and falling on a smooth swell. I was a quarter of a mile from land. I tried to row, but could do little more at first than make the boat spin round and round. After a time I did better, but it still seemed as if I should never reach the shore. It was slow, tiring work and I began to suffer from thirst and the heat of the sun. Then, as the boat lifted on a wave, I saw the *Hispaniola* under sail not half a mile away.

Someone must have set the sails, but nobody was steering and the ship was swinging this way and that, sometimes stopping altogether as she ran into the wind.

"Well," I thought, "if the guards are drunk I might get on board and return the ship to her captain. I can at least try."

But first I had to reach her. With the awkwardness of my boat this was far from easy, but at last I was near enough to see the waves boiling white under her side. The next moment she lifted and heeled towards me. She was almost on top of me. I jumped and grabbed a rope, and as I did so my boat went under water

beneath my feet. There was nothing for it now but to climb on board.

At a glance I thought there was no one on the deck. Then my eyes fell on the two mutineers who had been left to guard the ship. A man in a red cap lay flat on his back, his arms stretched out and his teeth showing through his open lips. Israel Hands sat with his back against the rail, his chin on his chest, his hands lying open before him on the deck, his face as white as a candle. Both, I felt sure, were dead. There was blood upon the deck-planks.

As I stood there looking round me Hands turned a little. Remembering all that I had heard in the apple barrel, I felt no pity for him.

"Brandy!" he gasped. "Give me brandy."

I went down into the cabin. The place had been wrecked. I found some fruit and a piece of cheese, drank some water, and then took Hands his brandy. He gulped at it greedily.

I sat down to eat. He asked where I had come from.

"I've come to take possession of this ship, Mr Hands," I said sternly. "You'd better look upon me as your captain."

"I expect you'll want to get ashore, Jim," he answered. "Suppose we talks."

"Say on, Mr Hands," I told him.

"Captain Hawkins," he said, "unless I helps you, you'll never sail her. Now, look here, you give me food and drink, and a bit of rag to tie up my wound, and I'll tell you how to sail her. I've no choice—I can see that. I've lost and you've won."

"Yes," I agreed, very pleased with myself, "and we're not going back to the old anchorage. We'll make for the north of the island and run her ashore."

Hands agreed. I tied up his wound, a great cut in the leg, and in a few minutes I had the *Hispaniola* sailing easily before the wind. Hands, who now looked a lot better, watched me with a strange smile on his face.

I sailed on until we came to a little bay at the north of the island. We had to lie off the entrance till the tide rose higher. While we waited we talked. Presently Hands asked me to go below and get him a bottle of wine.

"He has brandy already," I thought. "He wants me off the deck for some reason of his own."

I agreed to go. As soon as I was out of his sight I took off my shoes, and returned without a sound to a place just behind him where I could watch him without being seen. I understood then. I saw him crawl towards a coil of rope and pick up a blood-stained knife that was lying inside it. He put it under his coat, and then crawled back to his first position.

This was all I needed to know; I must be on my guard. He still wanted to get ashore, however, and I thought that I should be safe till we got there. I put my shoes on and went back to him with his bottle of wine. Then, with his help, I steered the ship straight in towards a smooth, sandy beach.

I was so occupied with this that I forgot the danger that hung over my head. I might have died instantly if something had not made me turn. When I swung round there was Hands halfway towards me with the knife in his right hand.

We both cried out as our eyes met. He threw himself forward and I jumped to one side. As I did so I let go of the tiller, which swung round and struck him across the chest. That stopped him, for the moment.

Before he could recover, I leaped across the deck, turned, drew

one of my pistols, took aim, and pulled the trigger. Nothing happened: the powder was wet with sea-water from my night in the open boat.

I had no time to try my other pistol. Hands, wounded as he was, came after me with surprising swiftness. I ran and dodged here and there about the deck, and it was all I could do to keep out of his grasp.

Suddenly the *Hispaniola* struck the beach and tipped right over to port. In an instant the two of us went rolling across the deck. I was on my feet first and ran, but he was right after me. I sprang into the shrouds of the main-mast and clambered up like a monkey, until I was seated high on the cross-trees. I glanced down and saw Israel Hands looking up, his mouth open in surprise and anger.

Now that I had time I put my pistols to rights. Hands watched me do this, an ugly scowl on his face. Then he also started to haul himself heavily into the shrouds, and, with the knife between his teeth, began slowly and painfully to climb. I could see that his face was twisted with the pain of his wound. I waited until he was halfway up, then called down to him, with a pistol in either hand trained at his head.

"One more step, Mr Hands," I said, "and I'll blow a hole in your head."

He stopped at once. I could see by his face that he was working out his next step. I smiled, quite sure that I was safe. He took the knife from his mouth and spoke.

"Jim," he said, "I've no luck at all. I'll have to give in."

Like a flash his right hand went back and something sang like an arrow through the air. I felt a blow and then a sharp pang. His knife had pinned my shoulder to the mast. In pain and sur-

prise I pulled the triggers of both my pistols, and dropped them at the same time. They did not fall alone. With a choked cry, Hands loosed his grasp upon the shrouds, and plunged head first into the water.

Feeling sick and faint, I lifted a hand and tried to pull the knife from my shoulder. My courage failed me, however. There was hot blood running over my back and chest. I began to tremble. The shaking did it—the knife held me only by my skin and the trembling set me free.

The sun was going down, and I was alone upon the ship. I made my way down shakily to the deck, where I found that my wound was little more than a deep cut in the flesh of my shoulder. I waded ashore and in good heart after my narrow escape I began walking back towards the fort.

Gradually the night fell blacker and it was all I could do to find my way. At last I drew near and went slowly, for I did not wish to be shot by my friends. It struck me that they were keeping a poor look-out. I came to the fence and crossed it, and no voice challenged me. I could see the remains of a fire before the house, and I got down on my hands and knees and crawled towards it.

When I came to the door I stood up. Holding my arms out before me I stepped into the darkness within. My foot struck something—a man asleep on the ground. He turned and groaned, but did not wake, and then my flesh crept as a voice spoke out of the darkness.

"Pieces of eight!" it said. "Pieces of eight! Bring me rum!"

I felt my blood freeze. The voice was that of Silver's green parrot, Captain Flint.

I had not time to flee. At the sharp tone of the parrot, the

sleepers awoke and sprang up. With a mighty oath, the voice of
Silver cried:

"Who's there?"

I turned to run, and a hand came out of the blackness and
took my neck in an iron grip.

"Bring a torch, Dick," cried Silver, and I knew that all was
over with me.

Chapter Twelve

In the Enemy's Hands

"So" cried Silver, "here's Jim Hawkins, by thunder! Dropped
in like a friend, eh?"

The red glare of the torch showed me that six of the pirates
were there, all glaring at me fiercely.

"Now," Silver went on, "I must say that I've always liked you,
Jim, and it looks as if you'll have to join up with Captain Silver.
I don't know where your friends are. Dr Livesey came with a
flag of truce and told us the ship was gone. And, by thunder, so
she was! Will you join us, Jim?"

"Let the worst come to the worst," I said, "it's little I care. But
let me tell you that you're in a bad way, and it was I who beat
you. I was in the apple barrel and heard you talk of mutiny. I cut
the ship's hawser, and I killed Israel Hands. If you spare me I'll
do what I can to save you from hanging. If you kill me, it'll do
you no good—"

There was a sudden growl from the pirates.

One of them drew a knife and I thought my last hour had

come. Silver, however, held the others off, though they stood up to him till he shouted them down.

"If any of you want to have it out with me," he cried, "you know the way. Let him that dares take a cutlass, and I'll see the colour of his inside! I like that boy. He's more of a man than any two of you rolled into one."

The next thing was that the men went outside to discuss it among themselves. The moment they were gone, Silver came close and whispered to me.

"They're going to throw me off, Jim, but I'll stand by you through thick and thin. You're a hair's breadth from death, but we'll stand together, says I. I'll save your life, if I can—and you save Long John from hanging if you gets the chance."

In another minute the men returned, and one of them slipped something into Silver's hand.

"The black spot," said Silver. "I thought so. You've finished with me, have you? Well, I'm still your captain till you speak your complaints and I reply."

"You've ruined everything on this voyage," scowled a man named George, "and now there's this boy."

"So I've ruined everything, have I?" cried Silver. "You all know what I wanted, and if that had been done, we'd have been aboard the *Hispaniola* this night—and with the treasure too, by thunder! As for the boy, ain't he a hostage? Kill him? Not me, mates. And didn't I make a bargain for you? Ain't the doctor coming to see you every day, and didn't I get this from him?"

And as he spoke he threw down the chart— the real chart that I had got from Billy Bones!—at their feet.

They leaped upon it like cats upon a mouse.

"Now," said Silver, "you lost the ship; I've found the treasure.

Who's the better man? And now I resign, by thunder! Choose what captain you like!"

"Silver!" they cried. "Silver for captain!"

That was the end of the night's argument. Soon after, with a drink all round, we lay down to sleep, while one of the pirates kept guard.

We were awakened in the morning by the arrival of Dr Livesey. He had come to attend a wounded pirate, and brought medicine for another who was ill with fever.

"We've a surprise for you," cried Silver. "We've a little stranger here."

"Not Jim?" said the doctor coolly. "Well, well!"

He gave me a nod, and then went on with his work. He must have known that his life hung by a hair, but he behaved as if he were visiting a quiet family at home.

"You must all take the medicine I've brought," he said when he had finished with the wounded man. "And now I wish to have a talk with that boy."

"Jim," said Silver, "will you give me your word of honour not to run away?"

I promised, and Silver said that if the doctor would go outside the fence he would bring me down to talk to him from the other side.

The moment the doctor had left, the men turned on Silver again. He waved his chart in their faces.

"By thunder!" he cried. "We'll keep the terms of our treaty till the time comes to do otherwise." Then he led me towards the fence.

"Go slowly, Jim," he whispered. "They might turn on us in a second, if we was seen to hurry."

He stopped as soon as we were within speaking distance of the doctor. Then he stepped back a little way and left me there alone.

"So, Jim," said the doctor sadly, "here you are at last. Now, this I must say, be it kind or unkind: you dared not have run off when Captain Smollett was well; and when he was ill, by George, it was a cowardly thing to do." I must confess that here I felt hot tears in my eyes.

"Doctor," I said, "I've blamed myself enough. If Silver hadn't stood by me, I should be dead by now. And if they torture me..."

"Jim," the doctor interrupted, and his voice had changed, "I can't let you stay here. One jump and you're out, and we'll run for it."

"Doctor," I said sadly, "I gave my word."

"I know, I know," he answered, "but I'll take it on my shoulders, Jim. Come on, now, jump!"

"No," I replied, "you wouldn't do it yourself. And you didn't let me finish. If they torture me I might tell where the ship is—in a little bay to the north."

Then I told him all my adventures.

"There's a kind of fate in this," he said at last. "At every step you've saved our lives. Silver!" he cried to Long John, "I'll give you a piece of advice. If you look for that treasure then look out for trouble too. Keep the boy close to you, and when you need help, shout for it. Goodbye, Jim."

He shook hands with me through the fence and walked off into the woods.

Just then a man hailed us from the fire that breakfast was ready. As we ate it, Silver sat with his parrot on his shoulder and talked on and on to build up the confidence of his men, telling them that they were soon to find the treasure. For my part, I felt very

sad and lonely. My chances seemed poor enough, and I could not understand why my friends had given up the fort and the map. I had little taste for my breakfast, and it was with an uneasy heart that I set out behind my captors on the search for treasure.

Chapter Thirteen

The Treasure Hunt

We made a strange-looking party, had anyone been there to see us; all in soiled sailor clothes, and all but me armed to the teeth. Silver had two guns slung about him, and his parrot on his shoulder, and held a rope which was fastened round my waist. Some of the men were carrying picks and shovels.

We went down to the beach, got into the boats, and rowed across the mouth of our old anchorage towards Spyglass Hill.

The party spread out as soon as we set foot on land. Silver and I followed behind the rest. Presently, from our left, a man began to shout, as if in terror. Shout after shout came from him, and we hurried in his direction. When we reached the spot where he stood pointing, we saw the reason for his cries.

At the foot of a tall tree a human skeleton lay, with a few shreds of clothing, on the ground. Its bones were picked clean and white, its feet pointed in one direction and its hands, above its head, in the opposite. I believe a chill struck for a moment to every heart. Then Silver spoke.

"Suppose this is here to point the way for us," he said. "Right up the hill there is our line for the gold. But, by thunder, it makes

me cold inside! This is one of Flint's jokes, and no mistake. Him and the six was here; he killed them, every man; and this one he dragged here and left to point the way."

"If Flint was alive " said one man, "this would be a bad spot for us."

"I saw him dead with these eyes," said another, "but if ghost ever walked, it would be Flint's. He died bad, did old Flint."

"Ah," said another, "he did that. he died shouting for rum, and singing his only song, 'Fifteen Men'. I've never like to hear it since."

"Come, come," said Silver, "he won't walk by day, you can depend on that. He's dead! Let's get on and find the gold."

We started off again, but the men kept close together and spoke softly. Fear of the dead pirate had fallen on them all.

We sat down to rest when we reached the high ground. The island seemed still and quiet, and the men whispered uneasily of Flint and the way he had died.

All of a sudden, out of the middle of the trees in front of us, a thin, high, trembling voice struck up the well-known air and words:

> "Fifteen men on the dead man's chest—
> Yo-ho-ho, and a bottle of rum!"

I have never seen men more dreadfully frightened than the pirates. The colour went from their faces; some leaped to their feet; some clawed hold of others; some fell on their knees to the ground.

"It's Flint!" cried one. "It's Flint's ghost!"

The song stopped as suddenly as it had begun.

"Come," said Silver, whose own lips were pale, "this won't do! It's someone playing a joke, you may depend on it."

The others began to take courage, and then the same voice came again.

"Darby M'Graw!" it wailed. "Bring me the rum, Darby!"

The pirates stood rooted to the ground, their eyes staring from their heads. Long after the voice had died away they remained still and silent.

"They were Flint's last words," moaned one of them at last.

"That fixes it!" gasped another. "Let's go!"

Still Silver was not so easily scared off.

"I'm here to get that treasure," he cried. "I never was afraid of Flint in his life, and, by thunder, I'll face him dead! And, come to think of it, it *was* like Flint's voice, but it was more like another I've heard. Yes! Ben Gunn's!"

"Yes, so it was," cried one of the men.

"And who minds Ben Gunn—alive or dead?" They all took heart at this. We went on rapidly. At last we came in sight of the tall tree beneath which, according to our chart, Flint's treasure had been buried. Silver was swinging himself along on his crutch now, and threw murderous glances at me if I held back. I had no doubt that he'd forgotten his promises to the doctor, and that if the gold were found my death would follow at once.

We were now close to the tree. The men began to run, their eyes burning in their heads. Suddenly we saw them stop. A low cry arose. Silver doubled his pace, digging away with the foot of his crutch like a man gone mad; and the next moment he and I had come also to a dead halt. Before us was a great hole. In it was the shaft of a broken pick, and several boards of rotting wood. There was nothing else. The treasure had been taken.

Each of the men stood as though he had been struck. But Silver acted instantly.

"Jim," he whispered, "take that, and stand by for trouble!"

He passed me a double-barrelled pistol. At the same time he moved, dragging me after him, so that the great hole was between us and the rest.

With oaths and cries, the pirates leaped into the pit and began digging and clawing at the earth with their fingers. One found a small gold piece, which was passed from hand to hand among them.

"There's your treasure!" roared one to Silver. "You're the man that never ruined anything, are you?"

"Dig away, mates," answered Silver coolly. "You'll find some pig-nuts, I shouldn't wonder."

"Pig-nuts!" screamed the man in a fury. "D'you hear that, mates? I tell you Silver knew this all along."

One after the other they scrambled up out of the hole and stood facing us. Silver did not move. He watched them, standing upright on his crutch, as cool as I ever saw him.

"Mates," said the same man, "there's two of 'em alone there, and I mean to cut their hearts out. Now, Silver——"

He was raising his arm and his voice, and plainly meant to lead a charge. But just then—crack ! crack ! crack !—three shots flashed out of the wood behind. Two of the pirates dropped and lay dead, their limbs still twitching. Long John fired two barrels of a pistol into another; and as the man rolled up his eyes at him in the last agony, "I reckon," he said, " that I've settled you."

The other three pirates turned and ran for all their might.

At the same moment the doctor, Gray, and Ben Gunn joined us, with smoking muskets, from among the trees.

"Forward!" cried the doctor. "Double quick, my lads. We must head 'em off the boats. "

Chapter Fourteen
End of the Voyage

I tore myself free from the rope by which Silver held me, and plunged after the others. We went at a great pace, sometimes diving through bushes up to our chests.

Silver made every effort to keep up with us, leaping on his crutch till his heart must nearly have burst. He was only thirty yards behind us when we came to the top of the slope and saw that there was no need to hurry. The pirates were not making for the boats, so we four sat down to breathe, while Long John, mopping his face, came slowly up with us.

"Thank you kindly, doctor," he said. "You come in the nick of time, I guess, for me and Hawkins. So it's you, Ben Gunn, is it?" he added. "Well, you're a nice one, to be sure. To think you've done me in the eye!"

As we went slowly down the hill to where the boats were lying, the doctor told me, in a few words, what had taken place. Ben Gunn was the hero from beginning to end.

In his lonely wanderings about the island, Ben had found the skeleton and found the treasure. He'd dug it up and carried it on his back, in many weary journeys, to a cave he had in the slope of a hill. When the doctor had learned where the treasure was, he had gone to Silver, given him the chart, which was now useless, so as to get a chance of moving to safety from the stockade to Ben Gunn's hill, there to be clear of fever and to keep a guard upon the money.

As soon as the doctor knew that I should be with the pirates when they found the treasure gone, he had run all the way to the cave to fetch Gray and Ben, leaving the squire to guard the captain. Ben, who was swift of foot, had been sent ahead to delay the pirates as best he could—and I have told you how well he succeeded. Gray and the doctor had arrived in time to drive off the treasure-seekers.

"Ah," said Silver, "it was lucky for me that I had Hawkins here. You would have let old John be cut to bits, and never given it a thought, doctor."

"Not a thought," replied Doctor Livesey cheerily.

By this time we had reached the boats. The doctor knocked a hole in the bottom of one of them, and we set out in the other for the little bay where I had beached the *Hispaniola*. Just inside the inlet, what should we meet but the ship herself, floating on the still waters of the bay.

The last high tide had lifted her, and here she was, having come to no harm at all. We got another anchor ready and dropped it in the water. Then, with the ship safe, we rowed to the nearest point to Ben's treasure-cave and, while the rest of us landed, Gray rowed back to pass the night as guard on board the ship.

The squire met us near the cave. To me he was most kind, but at Silver's salute he went red in the face.

"John Silver," he said, "you're a wretch and a pirate. I am told I am not to take action against you for the moment. Well, then, I will not. But the dead men, sir, hang about your neck like grave-stones. Their blood is on your hands."

"Thank you kindly, sir," replied Long John meekly, and saluted the squire once more.

We entered the cave. It was a large, airy place, with a little spring and a pool of clear water overhung with ferns. Before a fire lay Captain Smollett, and behind him I saw heaps of gleaming coins and a pile of long golden bars. That was Flint's treasure, that we had come so far to seek, and that had cost the lives of seventeen men from the *Hispaniola*. What it had cost in the past, what blood, what good ships, what lies and terror and cruelty, no man could tell.

"Come in," said the captain. "You're a good boy, Jim, but I don't think you and I will go to sea again. Is that you, John Silver? What brings you here, man?"

"Come back to my duty, sir," Silver replied.

"Ah!" said the captain, and that was all.

What a fine supper we had that night! And there was Silver, sitting behind us, but eating well, ready to spring forward when anything was wanted—the same polite, smiling sailor of the voyage out.

The next morning we fell early to work and moved the treasure to the ship. It was hard work and it took a long time. The three mutineers did not trouble us, though we kept a sentry on the look-out. Once we heard them singing, and it was plain that they were drunk. That was about the last we knew of them, except that when at last we set sail and were standing out to sea, we had a glimpse of them perched upon a little sandhill. They were screaming for us to take them on board. When they saw that we would take no notice, one of them raised a musket to his shoulder and sent a shot whistling over Silver's head.

We were short of men and set our course for a port in Spanish America, where we hoped to find a crew. We landed just before sunset, and I went at once with the squire and doctor to visit the

captain of a British battleship which lay at anchor in the port. Day was breaking by the time we returned to the *Hispaniola*— and by then John Silver was gone!

Ben Gunn had let him go, partly, he said, because he would never be safe as long as "that man with one leg" was still aboard. He had not gone with empty hands, having cut through a bulkhead and taken one of our sacks of gold coins. I think we were all pleased to be so cheaply rid of him.

The *Hispaniola* made a good cruise home. We got some extra hands, for five men only of those who had sailed returned with her.

All of us had a large share of the treasure. Ben Gunn spent or lost all of his in a matter of weeks, came back to us, and was given work by the squire.

Of Silver we heard no more. That dreadful seafaring man with one leg had at last gone out of my life.

That, then, was my treasure adventure, and no power on earth could drag me back to that accursed island. The worst dreams I ever have are when I hear the surf booming about its coasts, or start up in my bed with the voice of Captain Billy Bones ringing in my ears:

> " Fifteen men on the dead man's chest—
> Yo-ho-ho, and a bottle of rum!"

Illustrated Chosen Classics
——— Retold ———

Titles available in this series:

PhP
PETER HADDOCK PUBLISHING